SLEEPING WITH MY HUSBAND'S SON

N'DIA RAE

5 STAR LIT

CHAPTER 1

Katya

This is the life I've always dreamed of and I'd do anything to give it back. You really have to be careful with what you ask for, because you could get it and then some. Every single day I battle with the decisions I've made, and at this point I feel trapped.

Wind whipped through my shoulder length blonde bob as I tried to keep my wool shawl from scattering into the breeze. My sneakers stomped against the concrete as I made my way out of the parking garage toward the high end restaurant.

It was a little after noon and I was meeting one of my good friends, Markisa Randolph, for lunch. She called me to meet her at Eddie V's Prime Seafood, probably so that she could flaunt a new toy her husband bought her.

We were both married to ex-football players, who were just as generous with their money as they were their dicks. Between philanthropy and philandering, these men were very giving. And at this point I was over it, however, Markisa still accepted the gifts bestowed upon her from her husband.

Meanwhile, I had started donating my Buccellati trinkets and Gucci handbags to the local homeless shelter.

It's been 15 years of him cheating and he thinks that I'm still the 20 year old girl that he married. The young single mother who was so enthralled by a rich baller that I would do anything to keep him; including look away while his dick went on a United Nations tour.

My husband, Greer Song, met me while I was dancing in music videos and being a typical groupie. At that age I had stars in my eyes when he approached me for the first time on the set of a hip hop video. Scantily clad in a neon pink string bikini, I left nothing to the imagination when he sparked up a conversation with me over the shrimp platter off of set.

As tempted as I was to fuck him that night, I made him wait because I was thinking long term. I wanted the ring. No. I needed that ring. Getting wifed before I got ran through was the ultimate goal. If they get you while you're young you have a higher chance of getting you a baller with long money, versus a loser that's going to be broke in three years.

For example, see Mrs. Vanessa Bryant, she met Kobe during a music video shoot and got married to him when she was still very young. Rest in heaven to that king.

Then there are broads like Masika. She's so ran through the best she could do was pull a one hit wonder rapper with a gaggle of children.

Therefore, I did everything I could to become the wife of Greer Song. At 35, he was already on his way out of the league and had amassed a nice fortune. He had been married once but was divorced with one son. And in my mind, since he was done with the league, I figured he was done with the hoes. But, boy was I wrong.

"Hey honey!" Markisa shouted toward me as I walked near the restaurant. There it was, the new gift her husband gave her to apologize for his latest transgression. Whatever he did, it must've been heinous. Because sitting at the valet stand was a brand new dark sapphire hued Bentley Flying Spur; a quarter of a million dollar car.

Markisa stepped out of the driver's side wearing all white; cashmere leggings, a wool knit sweater and a pair of matching Balenciaga boots. She looked gorgeous, yet over-dressed. But that's how we lived. We'd both get dripped in the finest fashions to see if we could outdo one another. That's what happens when you're the housewife of a wealthy man.

Neither of us had jobs or businesses to run. My only daughter Zania is 19, while Markisa's 10 year old twin sons were always with their nanny if they weren't in school. Spa excursions, vacations, shopping trips and fine dining were our only outlets. But it was beginning to not be enough for me.

"Girl, why didn't you let the valet park your car?" Markisa asked as she handed over her keys to the attendant.

"Just felt like getting some extra steps in, I guess," I answered her as eyed her up and down. Markisa was a cute girl; petite, toffee complexion with a pair of green eyes. She recently dyed her hair auburn and it matched her skin tone perfectly. Seeing the warm color underneath the sunlight made me realize she made the right choice.

"That's so silly. Who wants to get extra steps in heels... Wait a minute. You wearin' sneakers? When did you get those tired ass Pumas?" she asked when she realized that I was dressed casually.

"I didn't feel like getting done up today."

"Shit, did you manage to take a shower?" she asked looking me up and down.

"Yes, I bathed! I'm just chillin' though."

"No make-up, yoga pants, a plaid shawl and sneakers? At least your hair is still fly, I guess. Should we just go into the mall and eat in the food court? This *is* Eddie V's." The judgement dripping from her tone irritated me. A part of me wanted to say fuck it and head back home.

"It's the lunch hour. Hardly no one will be in there," I replied as I rolled my eyes.

"That's a lie! Businessmen... having luncheons."

"Girl bring your ass in here," I snapped before heading toward the door.

"But wait did you see my new driving experience? Bitch, I can't even call it a car. That's an experience!" she exclaimed.

"It's gorgeous. But what did he do this time?" I smirked.

"I'll tell you after two glasses of Pinot," she answered as we stepped inside of the restaurant.

"Um can we get a booth in the back?" Markisa asked as she shadily looked me up and down. This shallow bitch was really ashamed to be seen with me, even though I looked fine. I just wasn't decked out to the nines like she was.

Moments later we were seated in a secluded booth where we both gazed down at the menus. I tapped my foot in anticipation for what she was going to tell me. It had to be something juicy if he splurged this much on her.

Despite the sun hanging in the middle of the sky and shining down brightly, the restaurant was dim. I squinted my eyes as they bounced down the menu to figure out what to order. It was useless because I knew this restaurant like the back of my hand. We've eaten here so many times, I've lost count.

"Good afternoon..." the server greeted us when he approached our table.

"We'll start with Pinot Grigio, the crab dip and the calamari," Markisa ordered before the server could even get a word out.

"Sure... I'll be right back."

Two glasses of wine later, our food had arrived and we both had a nice buzz running through our bodies. We'd already went over all the small talk and I was itching to hear what her husband did. Who did he cheat with this time? Perhaps he had another threesome? But given the magnitude of his gift, maybe he fucked her cousin. Both our lives were so drab that hearing her drama, might make me feel better about my own life.

"So..." I started, just as the server bought us another round of wine.

"Chile, this is my last one. I don't wanna crash my new driving experience!" Markisa spoke as she picked the glass up, bringing it to her lips.

"What the hell did he do? Why did he buy you that car?" I blurted out.

"You mean driving experience."

I sucked my teeth in annoyance.

"Fine... So you know how I've been laying low the last month or so," she spoke.

"Yeah. I thought you were just in a depression spell. Maybe you were off your meds again," I answered referring to her bipolar depression.

"Well yeah, I was depressed but that's because Shawn knocked up that white bitch that keeps his books!"

"What?!" I exclaimed. Our husbands cheated often but the one thing they didn't do was bring home any babies.

"Yeah, I was ready to leave him. I was not about to go through with that embarrassment. But she had a miscarriage at 8 weeks. Then she quit, of course for a large hush settlement. And he vowed to never cheat again. He said this was his wake up call and he promised that he wouldn't hurt me anymore," she said before downing the rest of the wine.

"You believe him?" I asked.

"Yeah! Why wouldn't I? He's never dropped this much cash on me at once. The car, these earrings and this tennis bracelet," she exclaimed while flashing her diamonds.

"Oh okay," I spoke as I sipped my wine.

"So what's going on with you and Greer?" she changed subject, fishing for drama to make her feel better about her life.

"We're good. I'm just in the middle of planning his 50th birthday party. He's been on his best behavior," I shrugged. To be honest, I stopped paying attention to how he moves. He was paying for my daughter's college tuition to Spelman and paying her rent in her own loft not too far from the school. I decided that being with him until she was finished was for the best.

"Where will it be?"

"At the house. It's going to be catered, casino and Gatsby themed. I'll be sending out the invites in a week."

"Ooooh girl! We should go to New York to shop! Shit or Paris. Me and you haven't taken a trip out of the country in a year." Markisa was getting wet just at the thought of spending money.

"No to Paris but we can do New York. I haven't been seriously shopping in a while."

She looked me up and down, "It shows."

"Bitch!" I laughed at her insult.

"What's going on with you? You don't look as fly as you usually do. You're a bad bitch. One of the baddest I know. The only one I consider real competition because Lord knows Angie is still tacky. Been with that baller for seven years and still buys the ugliest shit," she ranted.

"I just didn't feel like it today. You know? You don't ever feel like it's all too exhausting. Putting on a face. Getting dressed up. It's almost like that's all we live for."

"So! Bitches would kill to be in our shoes. Would you rather be working some 9-5 making only $40,000 a year? Shacked up with a broke nigga who's making you pay half of the rent while he cheats with your neighbor? I know our niggas cheat but at least they ain't broke," she hissed.

"I guess..." I said before eating the last of my lunch.

We talked a few more moments, before I rushed to the bathroom. Those glasses of wine were running through me and there was no way I was going to be able to make it home without relieving myself. After peeing, I washed my hands and caught a glimpse of my reflection in the mirror.

My honey brown skin was taut and clear; courtesy of my weekly facials at a lux spa. Recently I had my hair cut into a layered bob and dyed blonde with highlights. I had a diamond shaped face with high cheek bones. I was often complimented for my impeccable bone structure. Standing at 5'7, I was curvaceous and my body was fit. With no job, I had plenty of time to spend in the gym.

After I was finished I rejoined Markisa at the booth. "Well girl, I have to go pick up some weed before I relieve my nanny in a few hours," she announced after paying the check.

"Cool, I'll let you know about New York."

"Yeah I'll drive so that you can get a feel for a real driving experience," she giggled before walking away.

Shaking my head, I headed toward the parking garage. Moments later I was on the highway, stuck in traffic. That sunny sky transitioned into a grey mass. Those solemn clouds opened up like the Hoover dam. Rain rushed my window making it difficult for me to see.

As I drove bumper to bumper in the obnoxious traffic, I received a phone call. When I looked down, I noticed it was my doctor's office calling.

"Hello?"

"Hi may I speak to Katya Song?"

"This is Katya speaking."

"Hi Mrs. Song this Dr. Brenda Ali. I was calling to give you the results of your pap smear."

"Uh huh, I'm listening," I said as I turned on my windshield wipers. The rain had begun to pick up.

"Katya you have Chlamydia..."

As soon as the words left her mouth my heart sank to my gut. Tingling sensations washed all over my body and my vision became blurry. Before I knew it the front of my car was smashed into the back of another.

CHAPTER 2

Camden

If you would've told me that the son of a multi-millionaire quarterback and entrepreneur would be getting his car repossessed, I wouldn't have believe you. To most people being born to a man who could afford to buy anything in the world would be seen as a blessing. And to top it off, I'm his only son.

But nah, I'm sitting outside of my condo watching as the repo man loads up my red 2018 Porsche 911 on the back of a rusty flatbed. My candy apple coated baby was too damn fine to be on the back of a raggedy ass tow truck. Shit almost broke me down to watch it get wheeled away.

After three missed payments in a row, I was losing my most prized possession. I can't lie, it was my fault. A gambling addiction and a series of bad business deals gone wrong had landed me in this position. If it weren't for the fact that I bought my condo in cash two years ago, I'd probably be looking at foreclosure. At this point I was considering taking out a second mortgage just to play catch up with some of my other bills. But that was my last resort.

"I'm out!" Asia, my pregnant girlfriend barked when she appeared in the doorway with her baggage at her side.

A part of me was relieved to see her go. We weren't getting along and taking care of her was causing me to bleed even more money. However, I needed to figure my shit out for my baby girl that she was carrying.

"Aight." I shrugged before slipping my hands in my Nike joggers. A dark cloud moved in, covering the sun, shielding my face from the bright light.

"You are a fuck boy! You know that? Loser ass nigga. Got your damn car repoed! You better have some money for when this baby finally come. Bitch ass nigga. You not even willing to fight for me!" She barked while her pointer finger jolted toward my face.

"Look, if you wanna go, who am I to stop you? Shit, I got too much on my plate as it is."

"Fuck you Camden. Whack ass nigga. I'll be at my mama's house until you grow up and become a man," she spat before switching her ass away.

"Cool. Let me know when the next doctor's appointment is."

"Whatever. I should blast this all over Instagram. Show the world your little car getting taken away."

"Go ahead. You can do that if you want. But do you know how many videos I got of you with my dick down your throat? If you wanna play tit for tat we can do that."

"You would expose the mother of your child?!"

"All is fair in love and war, baby." I grinned flashing my smile.

"I hate you."

"You'll be back," I replied.

Naija was fine, but she wasn't worth the headache and she definitely wasn't the right one to impregnate. I had a feeling that for the rest of my life I would regret shooting up the club.

When I first met her, I thought she was a sweet good girl. Unlike the other bitches that threw pussy my way, she was different. She had this good girl next door type of charm. Didn't dress provocative. Didn't have a bunch of fake hair, nails or body parts. And even though she was an Instagram influencer, she wasn't posting thirst traps. Her father was one of the most popular preachers in the south, so she tried to be conservative. But once she started fucking with me and getting with my crew, she changed.

Even still, I knew she ain't want her naked pics or vids to leak. And I didn't wanna be that type of nigga but if she exposed me, I would expose her.

Anyways, after we met, we hit off. She was bad and real chill but she def wasn't wifey material. When she saw me, she saw dollar signs. I was good at making it look like I had cash. With over 200,000 followers on Instagram and the son of a well-known football player; I casted some pretty seductive illusions.

By flashing brands, cars, my crib and vacations; a lot of niggas thought I was paid. The reality was most of that shit was bought on credit, borrowed or rented. My ass was flat out broke. I had a few business deals that went bad and to top it off, I betted heavily on sports teams and played poker — and lost frequently. Now, the house of cards that I had built was tumbling down around me.

The tow truck and Naija pulled off at the same. My headache was gone but so was my car which caused heartache.

However, my man Cray Davey; a ball player had told me he would lend me one of his rides to keep up appearances until I came into some more money. He was the only nigga that truly understood what it was like to be disowned by your pops.

My pops... Where do I even begin. This nigga has been bitter about my mother since they split when I was just two years old. Apparently my mother cheated on him with a teammate and in the divorce took this nigga for a lot of his cash. He had to pay alimony and child support out the ass.

Which is why he made his current wife sign a crazy ass prenup.

Naturally, when I got older I sided with my mother. She made it clear that Pops cheated on her relentlessly and she slipped up once. I believed her. I've heard the stories about that man. He was legendary back in his day. But Mama ain't deserve that. She deserved the best. When Pops realized that I sided with her, he vowed to cut me off as soon as I turned 18.

He did pay for my college but after that he ain't give me shit else. Now at 28, I spent my time on the grind trying to make money without going the 9 to 5 route. Unfortunately, I wasn't as built to play football. He always blamed that on my mother's genetics. You would think since I ain't have the skill or build to play he would've helped me start a business. Nope.

This nigga had car dealerships, fast food joints and other investments but never helped me out. At this point he was better dead than alive to me. Pissed at the notion, I made my way back into my crib. The smell of rain hit my nose, letting me know it was time to go back in so that I could stay dry.

When I finally walked back into the penthouse suite I owned in Buckhead, I reached for my bong and small bag of the Skywalker OG that had been calling my name since I saw the tow truck out there ready to take my baby.

I looked around at the crib that I bought for myself back when I made some money moving weight. For a short while I was wholesaling coke and weed but got out quickly. I could feel the Feds were going to catch up with me at any moment so I made my money and got out. With that money I bought this crib, another whip that I wrecked, and invested in some businesses that went belly up.

The two bedroom condo, was decked out with the best decor I could afford at the time. Everything was white and black. Minimalistic. I didn't need color and shit in my crib. Even my pool table was black and chrome. Even the pool balls weren't colored.

The floor to ceiling windows allowed in copious light to wash over me but right now it was raining pretty hard.

I spent a lot of my money on my crib as well as some bad business deals.

First it was a porn app. That was a waste of $50,000.

Then it was the strip club me and my mans opened. It was going well until the place got shot up by some hood niggas. We had to close for liability reasons.

And finally it was another online idea; a weed subscription business. For various reasons, that shit didn't work out.

Now I was stumped. With very little to my name, I had no idea how I was going to make it. I felt like it was time to make an amends with my father and ask him for money but I knew he wasn't going to go for it.

I took several long pulls on the bong and leaned back in my plush leather sofa. I had a few paid IG posts coming up. I also had few different scams I could run. Cracking cards being one of them. I just hated doing illegal shit because there was always the chance I could get caught.

Just as soon as I began to get comfortable in my sofa, someone rang my doorbell.

When I looked on my phone to see who it was from my security camera, I quickly placed the bong down on the coffee table.

"Fuck!" I muttered.

It was Rayvon, the nigga I owed about 50 stacks to. I'd been blowing him off for weeks and now it was time to pay up.

"Open up!" he hollered from the other side of the door.

Quickly, I opened up and let him in.

"Wsup?" I asked.

"Nigga you know what's up. You got my money?"

"Shit's been tight. I'm working on it."

"You been working on it. Listen, you a cool dude but if I don't see some cash fast, I'ma have to slice that bad bitch you been running around with. And she carrying ya seed? I'll give that bitch a c-section. Keep fuckin' with me," he barked.

"Chill man. I got you. Give me a week to come up with 10 stacks, at least."

"15."

"15?" I asked.

"Nigga, I ain't stutter. Have my money. Better go ask Daddy to help you out," he said before swiping the rest of my weed off the table and heading out.

I kicked over my bong before crashing into the couch. I needed to figure out something and I needed to figure it out fast.

CHAPTER 3

Katya

A sprained wrist, a smashed bumper and a shattered spirit were all remnants of one of the darkest moments of my life. The damage to my heart was worse than the damage to my car and the person I hit.

Of course my insurance premium was going to be raised but that was nothing compared to the fucked up news I received that caused the accident.

Chlamydia. Never in my life had I ever had a STD, even when I was a video girl. I'd always made those niggas wear condoms. And I should've been making my husband wear condoms, considering how he got around.

I just thought that he was responsible when he was with his hoes, but I was clearly wrong. How could I trust him enough to wrap his generous gift of a dick up when fucking these other bitches?

Tear fell down my cheek, as I adjusted my body on the emerald chaise lounge chair in my personal room away from the bedroom we shared. In this mansion there were 9 bedrooms and since we didn't have any children besides Zania, one of them was my closet and another was my lounge area.

Inside the plush pink and emerald green room, was an entertainment set, a mini bar, a sectional and a chaise lounge chair, which was my favorite seat in the house. I had bought it from a vintage shop out in LA many years ago and knew that I wanted a burlesque inspired lounge room.

It was my sanctuary from the world. Whenever Greer left the house, I'd retreat in here with my bottle of wine, turn up some music and tune out my stress.

But today it didn't feel like a sanctuary. I'd just gotten back from the pharmacy to pick up my antibiotics for this disgusting disease that my husband gave me. My diagnosis made me grimace at the sight of myself in the mirror. Knowing that I had this infection in my body made me feel dirty and impure. I just wanted to hide away from the world.

Everyone expects for their pap smear to come back normal especially when you haven't been creeping. Hearing that I had Chlamydia was the most devastating news I'd ever received.

I reached down to the floor and picked up the bottle of Pinot and poured another glass before leaning back into the chair. Glancing down at my sprained wrist, reminded me that I was also in pain. Luckily, there were percs from when my husband had knee surgery earlier this year. That was probably the only time he's ever been in the house for weeks on end. The only time he hasn't cheated on me.

Even though I wasn't supposed to be drinking and taking antibiotics, I needed it. I couldn't bear a sober mind at the moment. Just as I pulled the glass to my lips, Markisa phoned me. Rolling my eyes, I placed the glass down and answered.

"Hey girl," I greeted her dryly.

"Hey! I heard about your accident. Are you okay? Why didn't you call me?"

"It was just a fender bender. I sprained my wrist. The Benz is fucked up and in the shop but I'm fine. The person I hit is apparently okay," I replied avoiding telling her about the STD.

"Oh okay. Well, do you want me to stop by later?" she asked, trying to be nosey.

"Nah, I just need to get some rest for the day," I replied.

"Okay sis. Take care. I'll reach out tomorrow."

"Thanks. Bye."

After we hung up, my stomach began to churn. Heat blazed throughout my body, causing me to perspire at the center of my palms and my chest. I rushed from the chaise to the bathroom where I threw up.

That's what I got for taking antibiotics with wine. When I was finished I slid to the ground and wept. I hated Greer for doing this to me and I wanted him to pay.

"Katya?!" I heard Greer's voice bellow through the halls.

He was out of town until just now. I'd called him and told him about the car wreck but not the disease he bestowed upon me.

I didn't even bother responding to him calling my name. There was a part of me that wanted to set this house of lies on fire with us both in it. He was dragging me down and I was letting him.

"KATYA!?" he hollered again as he busted into my room.

"What?" I answered in a flat tone. My heart raced in my chest, I heard his steps get closer. With my stomach still queasy, I made my way out of the bathroom to face him.

"How's the car?" he asked. This nigga was only concerned about the whip. Not that I was standing in front of him with a bandaged wrist.

"It's in the shop. Thanks for asking about me," I rolled my eyes.

"You aight?" he asked when he looked down at my wrist.

"Fuck no! Because of you not only have I smashed my car, I have fucking chlamydia!" I barked.

"What?" he stepped back underneath the overhead studio light.

Greer maintained his looks well. Even though he was about to be 50 years old, he gave men half is age a run for their money. While most athletes let themselves go after retirement, Greer continued to exercise and maintain his athletic figure.

And I maintained his diet. Even though we were wealthy, he preferred I did all the cooking. He ate mostly vegetarian but appreciated seafood from time to time. I was his live in cook, maid and sex slave. But he always needed more when it came to sex.

Standing at 6'5" he was built as if he were still in the league. Instead of a fresh cut face he now had a salt and pepper beard covering his mahogany complexion. To most he was fine as hell, but to me he was damn near a demon.

"You heard me. CHLAMYDIA!"

"You ain't get that shit from me. You been fuckin' around?"

"You know damn well that I ain't been fucking nobody but you. I got this shit from you. Who is she? Who's the bitch that burned you? I got into the wreck when my doctor told me. This is your fault!"

Humbled, he backed away from me and turned around. Sweeping his hand over his face he shook his head. I guess it finally hit him that he really did give me this disease.

"I gotta get tested," he stated.

"Yes the fuck you do," I hissed.

"It needs to be private. I don't want this getting out. I need you to call Davis," he said referring to his concierge physician. "And who did you go to?"

"Wow. That's what you're concerned about? You want to know who else knows? I went to the doctor for my routine check-up. So whoever works there, knows. It's against the law for them say anything, so don't worry."

"Aight, cool. Call Davis so he can get over here to do that test a.s.a.p. I'm gonna go take a hot shower. I'm worn out."

"Worn out from passing around your plague?"

"Katya I was really out of town on business. I got an opportunity to buy a stake in the New York team. This can really put us in the billionaire category within a few years"

"Are you that far gone? We aren't going to make it another few years if you keep cheating on me. You haven't even apologized!"

"My bad. It won't happen again. Just call Davis."

"You're a piece of work," I replied while rolling my eyes and walking past him. I left him standing in the room, while I made my way downstairs to call Davis.

"I'm sorry Kat. I ain't mean to give you no damn disease. I promise it won't happen again," Greer said while on my heels.

"It won't happen again? Are you done cheating on me? Because if not, I'm done with this marriage."

"I gotta go take a shower. When I get done, Davis better be on his way over here," he said before disappearing down the hall.

Frustrated I picked up the phone to call Davis. Embarrassment fell over me like leaves in autumn. My throat was dry as the Sahara as I waited for him to answer.

"Mrs. Song, what can I do for you?" Davis answered with flirtation dripping from his voice.

Davis' wife had died about two years ago, forcing him to raise his teenage daughter on his own. Since his wife's passing he's lightly flirted with me but it never went beyond that.

"My husband needs a test for Chlamydia and he's gonna need some antibiotics," I replied. Hearing the words leave my mouth made me gag.

"What as he gotten himself into now?" Davis sighed.

"Tainted coochie."

"Are you okay? Do I need to test you too?" he asked hesitantly. I could hear the pity hiding in his words. Even on the phone I wanted to run and hide in shame.

"I've already been tested. That's how we know he needs it."

"Okay. I'm on my way."

"Thanks," he replied before hanging up.

Too embarrassed to face him when he showed up, I grabbed the keys to the G Wagon and headed out of the house.

My trifling husband can deal with this shit on his own. I just needed to get out for a ride before I set that house on fire a la Left Eye.

CHAPTER 4

Katya

Sleep evaded me the next few nights and it was starting to show on my face. There was more baggage under my eyes than Hartsfield-Jackson and seeing myself made me cringe. After splashing ice cold water on my face, I brushed my teeth and got ready to start my day.

Breakfast for Greer. Finishing up the final decisions for his 50th birthday. And getting a facial were all on my to-do lists.

Honestly, if it weren't for the amount of money spent and invitations that had already been sent, I would've cancelled his party. However, I couldn't stand anymore shame or embarrassment so I decided I was going to go through with it.

Dressed in a lavender silk kimono robe, I floated down to the kitchen so that I could prepare breakfast. Two egg-white omelets with spinach, bell pepper and onion. Home fries. And fresh squeezed orange juice. I had half the mind to piss in his juice.

My thoughts raced in my mind as I considered leaving his ass. But I was virtually broke. And that prenup I signed would leave me with hardly anything. And even though I didn't need all of the luxuries he provided, I couldn't see myself going back to living in a small regular apartment like I did when I was a young single mother.

"Morning," he greeted, while disrupting my thoughts. He sauntered over to me as I fixed his plate. With his arms wrapped around my waist, he kissed me on the cheek. It had been five days since we'd both been on antibiotics and he was already acting like nothing happened. Meanwhile I was fighting the urge to kill him.

"Morn."

"Is that Swiss cheese?" he asked while taking a plate and bringing it to the breakfast nook.

"Provolone."

"Why didn't you use Swiss cheese?"

"What difference does it make?" I asked while shrugging.

"What's up with the attitude?" he had the audacity to say. I stared at him as if he had three heads growing out of his neck. He was shirtless while wearing a pair of flannel pajama pants. Seeing his flesh made me want to pick up a knife and drive it through his cold heart.

"Are you kidding me?"

"You still mad about the chlamydia? Look, I said I was sorry. We got medicine before it got bad. We straight."

"No we're not straight. Next time it could be HIV. How could you be so stupid and reckless with our lives. You don't love me. Nor do you respect me. You're not even going to bother to stop cheating, are you?"

Blankness fell over his face like a desk-top computer shutting down from being unplugged. The silence was so loud it was causing my ears to ache. He really didn't give a fuck.

"Wow. Wooow. Unbelievable."

"What the fuck do you want from me? Huh? I give you everything you want. You ain't gotta work. Shit, you want the Flying Spur like your girl got? You want pink diamonds? You wanna go to Tahiti? I'm out here grinding to make us a billionaire super couple. And you trippin' about some hoes I fucked. They don't get shit out of me but dick. I don't even care if they cum or not," he said to me.

The words slammed into me like a train wreck. Dazed, my eyes fluttered as I backed away from the breakfast nook. Tears rushed my face as my bottom lip trembled.

"I can't do this anymore." The words seeped out my mouth.

"Do what? Stay rich and married?" he chuckled.

"Yes. I can't keep letting you take me through this," I whimpered, embarrassed that he was seeing me cry.

"Fine, file for divorce. You leave with what you came in with. And from what I can remember that was a fake Louis Vuitton carryon suitcase. You forget that I wifed you when you were just some video hoe that already had a baby by some dead-beat. I made Zania my daughter. I took y'all out of that mouse infested one bedroom apartment."

Everything he said was true. I'd wasted my years married to him and had nothing to show for it. Hearing it come from his mouth knocked the wind out of me. And if it weren't for the antibiotics, I would've been pouring myself a stiff drink at 9:00am.

"You just expect me to look the other way?" I asked.

"Yeah like you have been for the last 15 years. Look, I ain't nearly as bad as I used to be. That bitch that burned me? Better make sure I'ma make that bitch pay. And I promise to not fuck around in state anymore. And one day I'ma stop completely."

"Whatever," I muttered as I wiped my tears and turned away.

"You wasn't saying that shit when I paid for Zania's tuition. Or when you go swiping my card buying those silk robes and shit," he hollered after me.

Just as I was about to head back upstairs, I heard the front door open. Speak of the devil, In walked my daughter with a pair of large Chloe shades shielding her eyes from the sun. She sported a pair of light blue skinny jeans and a dark denim jacket while her long knotless braids were wrapped up in a bun.

"Hey Mama," she greeted as she pushed her way through the door. On her shoulder was an oversized Louis bag. Zania was just as spoiled as I was. Greer made sure that she was the flyest of all the girls she went to high school with.

He'd gifted her a brand new Porsche for her 16th birthday. And for her high school graduation gift, gave her a G Wagon. Zania never repeated outfits in high school, making her the envy of all her classmates. She had more than I could ever dream for her.

And to top it off, she was a smart girl. She was enrolled at Spelman for Biology because she said that she wanted to go into sports medicine. She wanted to be one of the league's top doctors. I couldn't lie, my baby girl had her head on better than I did at her age.

"Hey baby, what are you doing here?" I asked as she closed the door. Quickly, I wiped the tears from my eyes to hide that I'd been crying.

"Came to get my health insurance card."

"Are you okay?" I asked in concern.

"I'm fine. I just think it's time I get on birth control."

"Oh okay. It's in the office."

"Thanks. What's wrong with you?" she asked.

"Walk with me," I replied as I made my way to the office down the hall.

"Hey Z!" Greer appeared from around the corner, causing my stress levels to raise again. I heavily breathed as he hugged her.

"Can you put a shirt on?" I asked.

"Hey G!" she greeted him back, ignoring what I'd just said.

"What are you doing home?" he asked.

"Just needed to grab a few things."

"Cool, Let me know if you need anything?"

"Well, my girls and I wanna go to Aspen for winter break. Can you hook us up with a luxury rental cabin?"

I stood by and watched the exchange happen.

"I got you baby girl," he said before kissing her on the cheek.

Together she and I continued to the office. Enraged, I violently searched for her health insurance card. I slammed drawers shut and whipped out the card, tossing it to her.

"Mama what's wrong?"

"We had another fight..."

"About him cheating?"

"Yeah."

"You let him."

"What?" I asked ready to slap the taste of her mouth.

"You let him cheat. He only does it because he knows he can get away with it. It might be time for you to move on."

"When I get my ducks in a row, I definitely am."

"Until then, I'm gonna keep spending his money," Zania laughed before walking out of the office.

There was no way I could bring myself to tell her about the STD. I was too ashamed that it even happened. There was a part of me that felt tainted.

Since I was already in the office, I decided to settle behind the computer screen and get to work on the final touches for the party. The caterers, decoration and the casino rental had been booked already. The last thing to finalize was valet service.

After I made the last few payments and phone calls, I decided it was time to get ready for my spa appointment. Today I was going to a medical spa to see if I could get some fillers under my eyes because I was looking rough.

As soon as I got out of the shower, Markisa called.

"Hey KiKi," I answered with less tension than the last time we spoke.

"You sound better. Are we still on for our spa date?"

"Yep. I'm getting dressed now."

"Please, tell me you're not going to be looking like a soccer mom again."

"Bye Markisa," I ignored her before hanging up.

She was so shallow but at right now, I needed something to keep my mind off of my husband and this STD. Quickly, I got dressed in a pair of black skinny jeans, flat thigh high boots and a cream blouse.

I didn't bother with my make-up since I was going to be getting injections and a facial. Swiping my all black monogrammed Louis bag off my vanity, I made my way downstairs.

When I got there, Zania and Greer were in the living room talking.

"I'm gone. See y'all later," I called out to the two of them.

"Okay, Mama," Zania replied but Greer said nothing. Bitch.

Rolling my eyes I stomped outside and jumped in the G Wagon and made my way down to the spa. Markisa arrived about two minutes after me.

Today, I let valet park my car. I fully intended on spending as much of Greer's money as possible. It wouldn't make up for him cheating and burning me but it would make feel a little better.

"That's more like it," Markisa commented when we entered the lobby. She eyed me up and down in approval. We were wearing similar outfits but on her feet were a pair of leopard stilettos.

"Leave me alone," I laughed but as soon as we entered, my smile quickly shifted into a frown.

Sitting in the lobby was one of Greer's old conquests. Kelly Richie. She was some bitch that he slept with five years ago, knowing fully well that he was married. Now this bitch was married to a washed up actor from a 90's sitcom that does chitlin circuit plays.

When I stepped through the door her eyes wandered up to me before she smirked and returned her gaze down to the magazine she was reading.

"We don't have to stay," Markisa whispered as she tugged my arm.

"Nah, fuck that. I gotta get these bags handled. Besides, I heard her and her man's house was going into foreclosure."

"What?!" Markisa became overwhelmed with giddiness at tea.

"Yep."

We stepped forward to sign in for our appointments. So that Kelly could hear me, I told Markisa all about the foreclosure, letting that bitch know that I knew she was broke.

It was petty but at the moment it was all that I had going for me.

CHAPTER 5

Camden

Posted up against the cerulean Lambo that my man Cray Davey let me borrow, I snapped a few pictures for the 'Gram. My other homeboy Marco, took the pics so that I could stunt. Night Shade, a club out here, wants me to host a party in a couple of weeks. I could make 5 stacks from that party if I can guarantee to have ballers in the building. The club was going to negotiate their fees.

Cray had already told me he could do it. I need about three more ballers and that would bring the bitches in. But to do that I had to stay on the radar and front like everything was good in my world. Whenever I posted and got thousands of likes it reinforced the idea that I was the nigga to chill with in a club.

When Marco handed over my phone, I did a couple of edits before uploading the pic with the caption; "New whip, had to get rid of my old bitch." It was definitely me throwing shade to Naija.

"Whatchu gon' do about Rayvon?" Marco asked as he reached in his pocket for a blunt.

"I don't know. That money from the club is survival cash. Pay my bills and buy some groceries. I'm thinking about selling my Rolex Datejust. I can probably get about 11k for it."

"Damn, you love that watch. I remember when you bought it."

"I know man... Out in Vegas. That was a good night. That was one of the two times I had a Royal Flush. Shit was glorious."

"Maybe you should go out there and try your luck again," he suggested.

"I thought about it but I can't take that risk right now. I'm already in the hole. So right now, I'm letting the watch go," I replied.

"True. Cray cool as fuck for letting you hold his whip."

"Yeah we go back. He's like a brother to me." It was true. We'd grown up together. Both our parents were professional athletes but his father wasn't too involved either. Our moms clicked and we were raised together.

Cray was doing really well by being a professional basketball player. That nigga was making over $5 million a year. He often looked out for me and I appreciated it.

"Why don't you just ask him for the money so that you can get Rayvon off your back."

"Nah. I'm gonna handle it on my own," I replied.

The reality was, he'd already bailed me out multiple times. I couldn't fade asking him for help again. I had to figure this shit out on my own.

As Marco and I continued to talk, the mail lady pulled up and entered my building. Her ass was looking good in those blue uniform pants. Marco and I both turned around to look.

"Aye I'm gonna holla at you later. I gotta go handle some business," Marco said to me before dapping me up.

"Bet," I replied before walking back into the building. Before I went up to my condo, I stopped and checked the mail. Secretly I hoped there would be a check in there but I knew better. There was something else tucked between the bills and Chinese carryout menus; an invitation to my father's 50th birthday party.

"The fuck?" I wrinkled my nose before hopping on the elevator to go back upstairs.

I opened the casino themed invitation and read it to myself. *You are cordially invited...*

Since I'm his only son, you would think I would get a call rather than this generic invite. But whatever, I tossed it in the trash. There was no way I was coming to celebrate that man. That nigga hasn't celebrated my birthday in years. In fact, he only ever texts me on my birthday. Fuck him.

Agitated, I picked up the phone and called my mother to tell her about the party.

"Hey baby, what's up."

"I just got an invite to my father's 50th birthday party," I stated flatly as I leaned forward and pressed my elbows into my marble countertop.

"Ha! I guess his little wife is throwing it. You should go."

"For what?" I asked while shaking my head.

"You need to talk to him. He's your father. Ask him for money. I know you over there sick about your Spyder."

"Yeah. Most definitely. I just... he always says no."

"That's because you don't ask the right way. Come up with a business plan and ask him for money that way," she suggested.

"Yeah that might work."

"I know it will. Trust me. If he sees that you're being responsible and handling your business, he'll give you some money. You just have to frame it as an investment."

"True. I'll try that."

"Good baby. What else is going on?" my mother asked. I told her about Naija and our breakup.

My mother and I were close. Even though it's been years since they've been divorced, she hasn't remarried. I used to think she was waiting to remarry until her alimony ran out which was a smart move on her part. She made sure to milk my dad for all that she could. But by this time she wasn't collecting it anymore. She had her own even planning business.

After we finished talking, I went to grab my watch and headed uptown to this jewelry shop that I knew would buy it.

It was going to be tough to part with my watch but not as bad as it was to watch my whip get towed away.

"You sure you want to part with this? It's a nice watch?" Bruno, the jeweler asked.

"Yeah there's something else I'm eyeing. Besides, I got a lot of wear out of this one. Time to move on," I lied as I leaned against the counter.

"Cash?" he asked.

"You got that much in cash?" I asked.

"Sure do. Let me draw up the paperwork," he said before turning away.

While he got everything together, I scanned the jewelry throughout his shop. A lot of people came here to sell their jewels when they got into a bind and then he resold them for profit.

Moments later Bruno returned with cash in his hand and the paperwork. After everything was complete, I made my way to my whip and called Rayvon.

"Sup boy?" he answered the phone.

"Got that 10 stack for you. Where you at?"

"At the crib. Slide through," he replied.

"Cool I'm on my way."

I hopped back in the whip and made my way to East Atlanta to catch up with Rayvon. The entire drive, I couldn't stop thinking about how I bad I was doing financially. My mother had a point though. My father might be more willing to give me cash if it were for a business. That would be some serious work to come up with a business plan within a week. However, I had a few ideas floating in my mind.

Eventually, I parked outside of his apartment. With the cash tucked in my Gucci fanny pack I marched toward his door.

After two knocks, I heard Rayvon holler, "it's open."

But when I pushed the door in, I instantly regretted. I wanted to throw the money on the floor and run back to the car.

This nigga Rayvon was sitting on the sofa with another nigga on his knees sucking his dick.

"Bruh what the fuck. Call me later," I barked before turning around and heading out.

"Nah fam. Give me my money. Ay boy get up for a sec," he said to the nigga on his knees.

My back was turned to the both of them. With one foot out the door, I really wanted to bolt the fuck out of there.

"Aye, close my door," Rayvon instructed.

Reluctantly, I shut the door but still didn't turn around. I was not with that gay shit. If I saw another nigga's dick, I might have to say fuck it and fight. I'd rather die than to ever witness the shit again.

I could hear Rayvon zip his jeans, making me cringe even more.

"Where the money?" he asked.

"Right here." I still didn't want to face that nigga. There was no way I would ever look at him the same again. After all the bad bitches I seen this nigga pull, he out here getting his dick sucked by another man. Disgusting.

"Give it to me."

"Bruh, you gotta correct your language. I ain't giving you shit."

"Nigga..." he replied.

Slowly I turned around, whipped out the money and extending my arm. I ain't even want that nigga to close to me. I didn't want that gay shit in my aura field.

He grabbed the money from my hand and counted while nodding his head. "Cool. Good job Bro. You bought yourself some more time. Thanks for coming through. You tryna get in on this?" he asked pointing to the back room. I'm assuming that's where his boyfriend was.

"Fuck nah."

"Tyshawn suck dick better than a bitch."

"I'm good," I answered while shaking my head and running out of his apartment.

In a rush, I headed back to my car. My heart banged in my chest and my stomach did more flips than Simone Biles. I could feel the vomit reaching for my throat, but I took several deep breaths, hoping I didn't fuck up this car. I couldn't afford to waste money getting Cray's whip detailed.

After a few deep breaths, my heart calmed down and I started my car. I wished I could bleach my eyeballs to get that horrible image out of my head. The only thing I could do now to block it out was get a bottle Cîroc and some Afghan OG.

CHAPTER 6

Katya

"You okay?" my hairstylist, Latonia, asked me seemingly out of the blue.

"Yeah, why?" I replied.

"Because you ain't hear a word I just said. But I'm done with your hair now. And you look fabulous."

"Thanks," I dryly responded while looking up into the mirror.

Latonia stepped away to grab some spray out of her bag as I stood and eyed my hair closely. My blonde bob was shaped in beautiful amber finger waves that fit perfectly for my husband's party tonight.

With only two hours before start time, Latonia did her thing. A smile crept it's way on my face after I had been sitting in frustration the entire time she styled me. My mind had been stuck on my husband's infidelities and how I was stuck in this marriage.

"Why do you seem so down. This party is about to be lit! When I came in and saw the decor, I was almost mad at you for not sending me an invite," she laughed.

Latonia and I weren't that close. She'd only done my hair a handful of times, so, there's no way that I was inviting her to my husband's birthday party.

"I just have a lot on my mind," I answered.

"True. Well soon you can get some liquor in your system and forget all about your worries. Let me see your dress!"

"It's right there." I pointed to the dress hanging on my clothes rack. It was an off the shoulder rose gold sequin mermaid fitting dress that I had designed by a local designer. She did the damn thing. The dress fit me immaculately, yet I wasn't excited about wearing it. I had zero excitement for this party all together.

"Hey you ready for me?" I heard my make-up artist tap lightly only door.

"Yeah, Tyshawn come on in," I called out to him.

"Hey Ty!" Latonia greeted him.

Ty had been doing my make-up for special events for a couple of years and had introduced me to Latonia.

"Well, she's all yours. I'm heading out," Latonia announced.

"Send me the Cash App request so I can pay right now," I said while pulling out my phone.

Immediately I sent her $500 for the hair. It was $400 for the style and house call but I always give large tips.

"Always such a generous tipper. Have fun tonight. And cheer up because I know once your husband sees you in that dress he's going to be all over you."

The thought of that made me cringe but I managed to fake a smile. "Thanks girl. 'Til next time."

"Hunty! Your hair is laid for the Gawds!" Tyshawn commented as he eyeballed the beautiful waves.

"Latonia is truly an artist." I smiled.

"Who you tellin'?! She ain't got shit on my artistry though. I'm about to beat that face. You are a gorgeous woman but I'm gonna elevate you to goddess status!"

"I know you will."

"So what's been going on? I heard you were in a car accident."

"I sprained my wrist but it's fine now," I said as I extended my arm. After a week of icing and being bound it was back to normal. I was finally off the antibiotics and I intended to heavily drink to get through night.

"Oh chile... I'm glad you didn't mess up that pretty face of yours," he said as he began my make-up.

Within an hour Tyshawn was finished with my face. After I paid him, I finally got dressed. With the sparkly dress, I decided to keep my jewelry simple to not overpower the look. A pair of champagne colored school open toe stilettos and cream colored mink stole complimented the look.

Gazing at my reflection, I smiled because I did look good. From head to toe, I would definitely be a showstopper tonight. The merlot stained lipstick went perfect with the whimsy eyelashes that Tyshawn placed on me.

"You look exquisite," I heard Greer say from the doorway.

When I turned and looked at him, I noticed how suave he looked this evening. He sported a tuxedo with a white jacket. His cologne wafted toward my nostrils, intoxicating me but as he stepped closer I was reminded of who he really was.

"You are wearing that dress," he whispered with his deep voice melting into my ears. He wrapped his arms around my waist and pulled me in close while nestling his face in my neck.

"Thanks." I broke away from his grip while shaking my head.

"You can't be still mad at me."

"Well, I am."

"I told you I was changing. Don't fuck up my night. You did a good job planning it, but don't mess it up with an attitude."

"I'm always on my best behavior," I said while turning toward the Xanax sitting on my vanity.

"Good, I appreciate you. And I got you something," he said.

After I popped the pill in my mouth, I turned around to see what he was talking about.

In the palm of his hand was a black Bulgari jewelry box probably containing something that would blind me.

"What is that?" I asked.

"Open it."

As soon as I took it out of his hand, I opened the box and lo and behold there was a beautiful diamond tennis bracelet. Unfortunately it looked similar to the tennis bracelet he gave me six years ago when I caught him in a menage trois. Instead of bringing that discretion up I said, "thank you."

"You're welcome. Check you out. Getting a gift on my birthday," he laughed as he pulled me in for a kiss but I dodged him.

"You can't mess up my make-up baby."

"My bad. I'll see you downstairs but I'm kissing that lipstick off after the party," he said before heading out.

I rolled my eyes at the notion. There was no way that I was sleeping with him tonight. Hopefully, he would be too drunk to even try.

Two hours and several glasses of champagne later, I was having a ball. The poker tables were filled with players, meanwhile several people crowded the bar. Everyone look gorgeous in their tuxedos and their satin and sequin dresses.

"Girl, you look good. I ain't mad you didn't want to go shopping with me," Markisa said as she neared me with a glass of champagne held in her clutch.

"Yeah, I had too much going on. The car accident... then I had to finish planning for this. You did alright by yourself," I commented. She was wearing a silver satin dress and a pair of white open toe shoes with ostrich feathers around the ankles. Diamonds dripped from her ears, wrists and neck. Shawn must still be feeling guilty to keep splurging on her this way.

"It's all good. Look at Zania," she said pointing to my daughter who was in the cut with a couple of her friends from school.

"She's gorgeous, right?"

"Yes! And aren't you glad she's out your house? I can't wait for the twins to get that age."

"I kind of miss her sometimes," I replied.

Ever since Zania went away to school we hadn't been as close as we once were. Something shifted when she graduated high school but I guess that's what happens. All teenagers go through that phase where they grow apart from their parents.

"Wait is she drinking?" Markisa asked.

"Yeah, and I been watching her all night. This has to be her fifth glass."

"Is she driving?"

"Let me go find out."

As I stepped away to ask Zania if she were driving, Davis approached me. I'd been avoiding him all night because I was embarrassed that he knew about me having Chlamydia.

"Katya, you look stunning tonight," he complimented me. Davis was the opposite of Greer. Greer had smooth mahogany skin while Davis was caramel complected. Standing at about 6 feet, he wasn't as tall nor as built as Greer but he was still very attractive. Chin hair and a mustache adorned his creamy face.

"Thank you Davis. You're not doing so bad yourself. Where's your date?" I asked to create more distance between us.

"She's over there playing another round." He pointed to the table. "I just wanted to check on you. See how you were doing. You're surely a strong woman for putting this on despite everything."

"Thanks, I gotta check on my daughter. I hope you and your date have a great time," I smiled while patting his shoulder.

Moments later, I was standing in front of my daughter. "Zania, who's driving?" I asked.

"I am. Greer told me I'm not allowed to let anyone drive my car," she replied as her words slurred.

"You're drunk. You're staying here tonight."

"No I'm not!" she blasted back at me.

"Yes you are. You are already slurring your words. Just stay here. Your friends can sleep in the guest rooms. If you drive like that, you'll get in an accident."

"Is that what happened to you? Were you drunk and that's why you fucked up your car?" she had the audacity to say to me.

Instantly flashes of my doctor calling and me running into the back of the car crossed my mind. A part of me wanted to slap Zania across the face because if she'd known what I sacrificed so that she could have that car, she would shut her damn mouth.

With a smirk on her face, she took another sip from her glass. Quickly, I snatched her clutch out of her hand and walked away.

"Ma, what the fuck?!"

"You're not driving. Shut up and don't embarrass yourself," I replied as I continued away. But by then tears were welling in my eyes.

How long was I going to be able to keep up this deception? Just so that my spoiled daughter could have the life she'd always dreamed of. How long was I going to let Greer disrespect me? I wish there was a way I could make him feel my pain or worse. I had never cheated before but that was about to change.

I wanted to cheat on him with someone that I know would hurt. Someone that would make him want to die if he knew about it. I wanted him to feel the pain, despair and shame that I felt.

With my thoughts racing like a horse at the Kentucky Derby, I stepped away into the kitchen where I slammed Zania's clutch on the counter. There was a bottle of gin in the cabinet that I needed right now. It was the only thing that would stop the tears from fucking up my make-up. I couldn't undo all of Tyshawn's amazing work.

"Hey... Katya?" I heard a voice from the doorway of the kitchen as soon as I knocked a double shot of gin down my throat.

As the warmth spread in my chest, I turned around to see who was calling me. Standing there was Camden, Greer's only son. It was rare he came around, but I felt it was only right that I invited him to his father's birthday party. Their relationship was strained but I hoped one day they could figure it out.

"Sup Camden. What are you doing in here? The party is on the other side where the pool and veranda are.

"Yeah, I know. I just needed a place to charge my phone away from everybody. I ain't want one of those drunk muhfuckas to take my shit when they left."

"Makes sense."

"You straight?" he asked when he noticed my watery eyes.

"No..." I blurted out. I thought about how my daughter and my husband didn't respect me.

"Hey what's wrong?" he asked as he neared me.

Camden didn't look like his father, instead he looked like his mother. His skin was the color of burnt sugar. His skin was lighter than his father's and he had a pair of green eyes like his mother. A thick beard covered his handsome face and was complimented by a beautiful white smile. To his father's chagrin, Camden was decorated with many tattoos. None were on his face but he did have one on his neck and down his arms. Who knows where else, I'd never seen him naked before. But the way his cologne was smelling, made me want to catch a glimpse.

Snap out of it Katya, this is your husband's son, I said to myself. But for some reason, I wanted to tell him all about his trifling ass daddy. I knew that Camden didn't like his father and somehow I knew that he wouldn't care if I bashed him.

"I can't take this shit anymore." It was the liquor talking. Normally, I was good with biting my tongue but between the Xanax, champagne and gin I was speaking my mind.

"Can't take what?" he asked as he neared me. His deep voice wafted to my ears.

"Nothing... I'm sorry for even bringing it up to you. You can charge your phone right there. Enjoy the party. I'll be back out there in a second."

"Talk to me Katya. I mean... I know we ain't never been tight before but you shouldn't be upset right now. Like, I only came cuz you invited me, you know. I think that was nice of you. You always shown me love but because of how I felt about my father I kept my distance. You can talk to me."

"It's his cheating. He's just getting worse and worse..." the liquor loosened my tongue. Thankfully not enough to admit to having Chlamydia.

"Damn. Yeah that nigga. He took my moms through it. Why do you stay?" he asked.

I threw my hands up as if I were presenting the house.

"You can do better than that nigga. You can do better than this. That's my pops and he selfish as fuck. He just need a taste of his own medicine. That nigga always controlling the situation and manipulating people with money."

"I know. I feel sick because I keep letting him."

"You just gotta come up with a way to beat him at his own game. And just know you got an ally in me. To be honest, I only came here to ask him for money," Camden confessed.

"Good luck with that," I laughed while shaking my head.

"Ha! Thanks. But I already know how that's gonna go down. I gotta try anyway. But you and I should catch up one day. Just one on one."

"We can do that," I smiled.

Camden and I were closer in age than me and Greer. Camden was 28 while I was 35. When Greer and I first got married Camden was 15. At that time he was going through his rebellious teenager phase and really hated his father for remarrying. I don't blame him.

"Can I have my purse back?" we were interrupted by Zania's voice.

"I'll catch up with you later Katya. Wsup Zania?" he greeted my daughter but barely looked at her on his way out.

"Hi," she flatly responded.

"What was that about?" I asked noticing the tension between the two of them.

"He's a petty bitch. He threw this party a few weeks ago at this club. Clay, Shemar, Chase and a bunch of other ballers were going to be there. Me and my girls weren't on the list and since we were under 21 we couldn't even pay to get in. I DM'd him to see if he would get us in and that nigga said no." She rolled her eyes as she snatched her clutch off the counter.

"Whatever. You are not driving away from this house tonight in your condition." I said ignoring her complaint about Camden not letting her in.

"If I wanted to go home, I would. But I came up here to get my phone. When you took my whole purse, you also had my cell phone... dummy," she sassed before tossing the bag back down and walking away.

There was a part of me that wanted to drag her by her ponytail and beat her but I was too drunk to care that much. Besides Camden left me with a feeling I hadn't felt in a long time. He was definitely packing in the sex appeal his father had, even though he didn't look like him.

I had the urge to fuck him. If I could fuck Camden and run off with a good chunk of Greer's money, that would leave me satisfied. He'd be floored to get a taste of his own medicine. But it would be worse. Me fucking his son, in the bed that we shared. I knew it was wrong but I didn't care. Greer had driven me to that point.

Him and my spoiled brat. I would divorce Greer and take his money and leave her with nothing. But I was just wishful thinking. There would be no affair with Camden, Davis, or any other man. And since I loved my daughter despite her bitchiness, I would stay with Greer until she was done with school. But by then, she'd be on her own.

Frustrated, I took another double shot of gin before rejoining the party.

CHAPTER 7

C amden

As I strutted down the hall to get to the party, I grinned to myself. The wheels in my head grinded as I began to think of ways to get back at my father if he said no to my business proposal. I could see the cracks in the ice of Greer and Katya's relationship.

Usually whenever we talked it was always very casual. Today was the first time she was ever vulnerable with me and at first it was strange. But as I watched her drunkenly tell me the truth about my father, I warmed up to her.

Her revelations about my father cheating made me laugh. What did she think was going to happen? That nigga was never going to change. He was going to be 97 years old and still trying to throw dick at old bitches in a nursing home. My pops had no chill. My mother would tell me all about his ways as I grew up.

She would always say, something is wrong with him. He has an addiction or something. I didn't understand it until recently. I had patnas that cheated on their bitches but not like my pops. Even in my relationship with Naija, I never cheated on her. Staying faithful wasn't hard for me to do. But for my father it was like trying not to breathe. The nigga simply couldn't do it.

The walk from the kitchen to the outside area took me a while. My pops' house was massive — which pissed me off about him. He had the money to help me out but he refused to. While him Katya and Zania got to live up in the lap of luxury I was struggling.

That's another thing, fuck Zania. That lil' bitch thought she was cute. I never let her into my parties if I have the power to do so. She wasn't going to be getting clout off of my name. It's bad enough of my father was fronting her lifestyle. Fly ass condo, expensive whip, college tuition and whatever else she wanted he gave. But for me, his one and only son, I had to ask for money with a business idea in mind.

It was bullshit. But if it didn't work out, I was ready to take drastic measures. I was at the point now, where I could do without my pops walking this Earth. And somehow, I felt like I could convince Katya to go along with it. The look in her eye was one of desperation and weariness. I could tell she was fed up if she felt comfortable blabbing to me about it. Maybe she'd see that he would be more valuable if dead.

With that ironclad prenup, she might just help me get rid of the man. But before I could talk her into killing him, I had to get in her head. I had to get in her bed. I could tell she might be prone having a drinking problem. She was drunk and slurring her words. It would be easy to get her in bed once we start hanging out together.

When I suggested that we should catch up, she was all for it. Clouding her judgment with liquor, drugs and dick was going to be how I get her to let her guard down. And once I started planting the seeds of getting rid of my father, we could enact a plan that surely gets us both paid.

"Hey Camden! Look at you lookin' like your father," my uncle Reggie said when I walked into the party.

In my opinion, I looked nothing like my father and everything like my mother. Uncle Reggie was my father's oldest brother. My pops had two siblings, Reggie and Gia. Gia was estranged though. She stopped fuckin' with my pops a long time ago and I never knew why. She calls me for my birthday every year and sends a gift though.

"Wsup Unc?" I said while giving him a hug.

"Nothing much. What you been up to?"

"Just grindin'. You know trying to set up my legacy to one day pass to my baby girl."

"Oh I forgot you got a little girl on the way. I ain't gon' hold you up. Go see your pops," he said pointing over to a poker table. He wasn't playing. Instead he was nursing a cognac while chatting up some woman I didn't recognize. He couldn't even keep his dick in his pants at his own party that his wife threw.

Shaking my head, I wandered over to him and greeted him. "Sup Pops," I said.

"Cam! Look at you looking almost as good as me." He laughed. "Excuse me Michelle, let me speak to my son," he said to the other woman.

"Happy birthday old man! The big five-o. I got you something," I said fishing in my pocket for a pair of cufflinks. I had recently came across them in my closet. I had bought them a couple of years ago but never wore them. I figured re-gifting them would be a good idea. It was my way of buttering him up before asking him for money.

"Thanks!" He took the box from my hand and opened it. "These are nice. This the first gift you've ever gotten me."

"50 is a milestone. Hopefully we can start over."

"Before you even ask me, the answer is no," he said before finishing the rest of his drink.

"What are you talking about?"

"You came here to ask me for money. Right?"

"What?"

"Listen son, I can read your mind. The answer is no. But why don't you play in the next round of poker. We'll play with real cash."

"I just came to say happy birthday. I don't want no money and I'm good on poker," I replied trying to avoid slipping back into my addiction.

"Oh aight. Why don't you come through later tomorrow. Since you're not here for money, I'd like to spend some time with you. How does that sound?"

"Sounds good."

"Cool. Have something to drink. Kick back and hang a while," he said before taking his place at the table.

It was confirmed, that nigga had to die. I wasn't sure how I'd pull it off but it needed to happen. Katya seemed vulnerable enough to give me some money and if not, I knew how to blackmail her.

After I broke away from my father, I had a few more drinks and chatted with some of his family. When Katya emerged back in the room, my eyes zeroed on her like a hawk to its defenseless prey.

From head to toe, she was gorgeous. Her body was on point, curvaceous and fit. Her face was gorgeous. And she was more stunning than any bitch in this party. That's how I knew my father was crazy. How could he repeatedly cheat on her?

I could tell from where I was standing that she was definitely feeling her liquor. Her eyes were low as was her energy. She slyly smiled as she talked to one of her girlfriends who seemed much more perkier than she did. That's when I realized, she probably likes to get high. Maybe it was weed. It could be pills. Either way, I was sucking her in and going for the jugular.

About an hour later, I escaped from party and headed back to my crib. When I got there, I crashed onto the sofa and undid my collar. With my bills mounding, I needed to act quick. Rayvon wasn't the only person I owed. Ugh. The thought of him made my skin crawl. I was never going to be able to get that image out of my head.

After hitting a Backwoods, I drifted off to sleep without any negative thoughts running through my mind.

"HOW WAS THE PARTY?" my mother asked as she chopped vegetables in her kitchen. She lived in a nice single family home out in Marietta. She was able to buy it with the money from my pops. Since she never worked, she knew that she couldn't go crazy. She bought a house that she could pay off quickly. And now the only thing she paid for was maintenance and taxes from the money that she made from her books, speaking engagements, and reality TV show.

She was on a reality show called ATL's First Ladies. It was a show that comprised of women who were wives of wealthy men in the city. My mother and one other were divorced.

"The party was cool. Katya did a good job. I can't even front. Too bad he treat her like shit," I said as I pulled the Heineken bottle to my mouth.

"What do you mean? Spill it baby," my mother said nearly salivating at the mouth.

"Man she was drunk as fuck..."

"Uh huh?" She placed the knife on the counter so that I could have her undivided attention.

"She confessed to me that he's been cheating and it's bad. It was so weird how she just blurted it out. She always been nice to me but she ain't never been open."

"Ha! That's what the lil' bitch gets. He is a dog and will always be a dog. I should've listened when his sister Gia told me to run in the other direction. But I was hardheaded. I guess it worked out. I got you and I have a fabulous lifestyle."

"Yeah... Shit's wild," I replied.

"So even at 50 he's still up to his dirty ways. Pitiful. Did you ask him for money for your business idea?"

"Nah. As soon as I approached him to wish him a happy birthday, that nigga said don't ask for money. It was strange. So I left it alone."

"Still ask him. Maybe, his birthday wouldn't have been the best time."

"That's what I'm thinking," I replied.

"Yeah try again. How's Naija by the way?"

"That's why I need some cash. I need to give her some a.s.a.p. to keep her quiet and satisfied," I responded. She was quiet about my broke status for now but who knew how long that would last.

"I can give you a little something. But it's a loan. I'm gon' need my money back," my mom said as she walked out of the kitchen to retrieve her checkbook.

Shaking my head, I looked up to the ceiling. Add this to the growing list of people I owe. I needed to get some money quickly.

CHAPTER 8

K atya

A Xanax and a glass of wine, slithered through my veins causing me to feel relaxed and detached. I laid on my sofa while watching television in numbness. No real thoughts came to mind.

Ever since the STD, I'd been numbing myself with wine and Xanax. The realization that I was stuck in this marriage for a while was becoming too much so I needed to stay high to endure it.

"I'm on my way out..." I heard my husband say as he passed me.

"Where are you going?"

"What's it to you?" he snapped back. When I glanced up I could see that he was dressed as if he were about to go out on a date. His beard was shaved and had a glistening sheen to it. Cologne filled the room when he entered and he had on a Rolex I had gotten him for his birthday a few years ago.

"Whatever." I waved him off. I was starting not to even care about what he was doing. I already knew he was about to go be knee deep some other bitch's pussy. It didn't even matter anymore because he would never be in mind again.

"That's what I thought. Just sit there and drink your wine. Don't worry about what I'm doing. We haven't fucked in weeks and you got the nerve to be questioning me."

"Have fun," I replied while thinking to myself after you burned me do you really think that I would ever let you touch me again.

Without saying a word he walked out of the door. It had been over a week since his party. That night he crept into bed with me and to tried fuck me. Even though I was wasted off the two bottles of wine and shots of gin, there was no way I was letting him touch me.

Shit, the next disease he may have given me was HIV. I wasn't risking it for his dirty dick. The night of the party made me realize several things. I was essentially his slave and there was no getting out.

Except there was something about Camden that night. I don't know where the overwhelming urge to tell about Greer's cheating came from. But it felt right in the moment. Something about Camden had peaked my interest and I wanted to fuck him to get back at Greer.

Camden probably hated his father as much as I did. Greer hadn't really been there for him and had cut him off as soon as he turned 18. There was a part of me that wanted to plot with Camden on killing Greer.

Just as I sat up from the sofa to pour me a glass of wine, I received a call from Markisa. I'd been distant from her since our lunch date. It wasn't that I was mad at her, I was just stuck in feeling numb. I barely wanted to be bothered with anyone.

"Hey girl," I answered the phone.

"What are you up to tonight?" she asked.

"Nothing. Television and chilling by myself."

"My God, you've turned into such a bore. How about I come pick you up in my driving experience and we go out tonight. We haven't been to the club in so long and I know you can use night out."

"Where did you have in mind?" I asked. Why was I even considering this? I'd much rather go upstairs and lay in my bed.

"Night Shade. Your stepson is throwing a party there. We should check it out."

"My stepson? Oh I'm good. I'll stay right here," I replied.

"Girl come on. There ain't that big of an age difference between you two. It's going to be lit. All kinds of ballers will be there."

"We both are married to retired ballers. You tryna snag you a new one?"

"No! I'm just saying it's going to be an A list event. Jordyn and Michelle are going to be there," she said to further lure me out. Jordyn and Michelle were our other friends. Jordyn was the baby mother of a basketball player and Michelle was the ex-girlfriend of a football player.

"Fine... I'll get dressed," I said, finally convinced that this was a good move.

"Good. I'll be there at 10:30," she said before hanging up.

When I glanced down at my phone I realized that it was 8:30. It was ample time to get dressed and to beat my face. If my husband wanted to go out to thot and bop, then so could I.

By 10:15, I had completed a full beat; contouring, eyelashes and a smokey cat eye. I sported my Alaïa leopard jumpsuit with a red leather belt around my waist. On my feet were a pair of matching red leather ankle boots. I took a few mirror selfies to admire how damn good I looked.

At 10:30 on the dot, she was calling me to come outside. I grabbed my red Birkin bag and skipped my fine ass out the door. My buzz had worn off, but that was okay. We were on our way to the club where I could re-up.

"Damn bitch, you got me over here questioning my sexuality," Markisa laughed when I sank into her plush leather seats.

"Thanks boo. You look fine too. And damn... these seats are buttery."

"I know right. I'm telling you, you're going to think you're gliding on air," she said as she pulled away from phantas-magoric prison of a home.

"I'm glad you called."

"Shit, I could tell you were probably up there watching Martin reruns and drinking yourself silly. We're gonna have a good night. Jordyn got a VIP section for us. The place is going to be packed with beautiful A-listers. And my God, I get a break from my twins."

"You always complaining about them twins."

"Because they're bad as fuck," she laughed.

Thirty minutes later we arrived at Night Shade, a new club in midtown. Markisa left her car with valet and we strutted through the VIP entry with ease.

Night Shade was a gorgeous club. It looked as if it were something from a Cirque Du Soleil performance. Aerialists dangled from the ceilings while women danced in cages off to the side. VIP areas were on both sides of the club while the dance floor was filled with people who had to pay $40 just to bump into people all night.

Together Markisa and I switched our fine bodies through the club until we arrived at Jordyn's VIP section. There were a few other women there that I didn't recognize.

"I'm so glad you came!" Jordyn said as she hugged me. She reminded me of the singer Sade. Light skin with a large forehead but beautiful, nonetheless. She sported a faux ponytail that cascaded all the way to the nape of her ass. It was dramatic but I was here for every inch of it.

"Thanks for having me. Next bottle is on me."

"No girl. Corey is paying for all of this. Just sit back and drink," she laughed.

Music blared through the speakers as I watched other people dance and have a good time. After two glasses of Moet, I was feeling relaxed. My buzz had returned and I began to feel my body sway to the music.

"Where are you going?" Markisa whispered to me when she saw me walking away.

"To the bathroom."

"Okay," she replied as if she were my mom. She was drunk off her ass. I had to roll my eyes and laugh it off.

"Ugh," I groaned as I made my way through the sea of bodies. There was so much space in VIP and I wasn't used to not being able to move freely.

"Katya!" I heard a male voice call my name. When I looked around, I saw that it was Camden dressed in all black with a few gold chains hanging off his neck.

"Hey Cam," I replied, slightly slurring my words.

"Whatchu doin' here?" he asked as he moved in closer to me. "You need a table?"

"Nah, I'm at one with Jordyn Johnson. I'm just going to the bathroom," I replied.

"Oh cool. You look damn good. Shit."

"Boy, go somewhere," I thwarted although I appreciated the attention.

"I'm just saying. My pops don't know what he got." His devilish grin almost sucked me in but I tried my best to ignore it.

"I said go somewhere."

"I'll go anywhere with you," he flirted.

"Leave me alone."

"I don't think you want that. Listen, I'm having an after party at my spot. It'll just be me and you. Text me and tell me you gon' show up."

"Boy bye," I waived him off as I continued to the bathroom.

"Seriously. We got some shit to discuss. I feel like we have a common enemy."

Then it hit me, he felt the way that I did about my husband. Just by him saying those words let me know that we could be allies in getting what we wanted. My husband needed to die. There was no way around it.

He was toxic to both us and we would both be better off with him. After I finished in the bathroom, I returned to the VIP section where I had a few more glasses of champagne.

"Who you texting?" Markisa nosily asked when I whipped out my phone to send Camden a text.

"Damn, you nosey," I replied.

"Just checkin' on you. I'm about ready to leave," she said.

"Your old ass tired?" I teased.

"Shut up. I gotta take the boys to karate in the morning."

"Cool, we can leave."

We stood up and said our goodbyes to Jordyn and Michelle. As we walked out I saw Tyshawn, my make-up artist, walking into the club with two beautiful women.

"Hey Ty!" I waved at him.

"Hey boo. You leavin' already? I guess your man want you home tonight," he snickered.

"Something like that," I winked back at him. "It's lit in there. I bet you'll have a good time."

"I'm sure I will," he smiled before walking off.

Tyshawn was about 5'8" with a lanky build. His skin was the color of toffee which matched his blonde fade that he sported. He was wearing a pair of stretch jeans and a Balenciaga shirt with the shoes to match.

When he walked away, I turned and waited for the valet to pull up Markisa's car. In the meantime, I sent Camden a text.

"I'll be home in 30 to pick up my car. Tell me where I can meet you."

"Meet me at 1:00am at my crib. I'll drop the location," he replied.

A sly smile stretched across my face. I got back in Markisa's whip and she drove me home. The entire time I contemplated, whether I was doing the right thing. But when I got home and saw that my husband still wasn't there. I knew that I had decided the right thing.

CHAPTER 9

Camden

Bad bitches filled the room to the brim. All of them were dressed half naked with baby hairs laid and cleavage showing as they bounced their round asses to the trap music blaring out of the speakers. It was funny to see how many of them came out tonight to meet the rich man of their dreams.

All of them had hopes of getting chose by a basketball or football star. Perhaps a rapper or producer. The shit was like hitting the lottery because in reality, maybe only one was getting chose to be someone's wifey. The other's would be a slide at best.

I stood in the cut, in a private VIP with Cray and a few of his teammates while bodyguards selected random bitches from the crowd to join us. Tonight I wasn't interested in any women. I was self-aware enough to know I couldn't afford no other women on my roster right now. Naija was enough.

The only thing on my mind was that American green. I just needed a huge lump sum and then maybe I would sit down with one of my white homies who knew the stock market. I had a few Jewish buddies that didn't really work, they just invested money and lived off the dividends. That's what I wanted, but the only way to get that was from my pops at this point.

I knew that with just a million, I could flip that into 10. And thankfully, Katya was down with the plan. I just had to get in her head a bit to really convince her. She was definitely going to be hesitant about killing my pops, but I knew between the two of us we could pull it off. The crazy thing is, I didn't even want all of his money. I would be happy with just a million. And that nigga was worth over $100 milli. I fully understood why Katya didn't want to leave his ass.

"Aye, why you ain't drinkin' nigga. You been babysitting that beer for over an hour," Cray said to me when he wandered over.

"I'm working. I gotta go back out on the floor and greet niggas. Gotta make sure everybody havin' a good time."

"I respect that bro. You a hustler for real. This shit you goin' through ain't gon' last forever. I know you gon' work it out. You always do," he spat before knocking back his drink.

"Thanks bruh. Hold up, I'll be back," I said when I looked down at my phone. It was Rayvon texting me, telling me that they were holding him up at the door.

I wanted to tell that gay ass nigga to go home. I didn't even know that he was coming here tonight. If I did, I would've put security on notice to block his ass. I let out a sigh as I took a swig from the beer bottle before placing it down on the table.

This nigga wanted to get into VIP but I didn't want him back there with us. He was trouble. And I wished that I never got involved with him.

Taking my sweet time, I walked to the front of the club so that I could let him in. I swear once I pay this nigga back, it was a wrap. We were done.

"Aye he wit' me," I said to the security guard, motioning for Rayvon to walk through. He had a chick and another nigga with him. I didn't recognize neither of them.

"This my girl Crystal and this my brother Rich," he introduced.

"What's up," I replied looking at Crystal while shaking my head internally. She was bad too. Reminded me of Rihanna with the short haircut. If only she knew that her nigga was out here getting head from another dude. The memory crept into my mind again, making me sick to my stomach.

"We in VIP, right?" Rayvon asked threateningly.

"Yup, with a few members of the ATL and Miami teams," I smiled.

"Oh shit! Thank you Von!" Crystal exclaimed as she pulled him in for a kiss. I wanted to vomit right then in there. Instead I turned around and walked back through the club with them on my heels.

But when we got deeper inside, I saw that gay nigga that sucked Rayvon's dick. He was surrounded by a couple of broads as he danced like a female. I shook my head and looked back at Rayvon to see if he saw his boyfriend. It was written all of over his is face, he definitely saw him.

Disgusting.

Finally, we made it back to VIP where the rest of the crew was. "Aye isn't that your boy that sells Molly?" Cray asked when he saw Rayvon.

"Yeah, is it cool if he sits here with us?"

"Hell yeah! He got any on him? We're tryna take those bitches back up to the room."

"Lemme check," I said before walking over to Rayvon. I picked up a bottle of Grey Goose and Ace of Spades for him and his crew.

"This is for you all. Those cups are clean," I said while pointing to the ground.

"Good lookin'. This spot is nice. When you think you gon be ready for that next payment though?" he asked while popping the cork on the bottle.

"Soon. I'm grindin' now. You know I'm good for it."

"Yeah you better be. I'd hate to have my girl Crystal slice up your pretty bitch's face," he said as Crystal smirked back. If only that dumb broad knew about her man.

"Nah I got you."

"Aye but lemme talk to you for a sec," he said while handing the bottle over to his brother.

"Wsup?" I asked when we moved over to a corner where no one could hear us.

"You remember that fag from the other night?"

How could I forget? "Yeah."

"He pressin' me for some white girl. Can you go drop this to him?"

"What?" I asked looking at him as if he had two heads growing out of his neck.

"Come on man. I normally wouldn't ask but this nigga been blowing up my phone. Tryna blackmail me and shit. When he saw me in here, he wanted me to bring him this."

"Fine but can you hook me up with some Molly right now?"

"Nigga that's gon' cost you."

"You got me runnin' drugs in a busy ass club. That's the least you can do."

"The least I can do is not come through your spot and let my chopper rain on you."

I tilted my head and looked at him as if he were out of his mind. I gave him a look as if to say, I know your secret, don't try me.

"How many pills you need?"

"10."

"I'll give you a discount. $100. It would usually cost $250," he replied.

"Bet."

After he gave me the Molly and the coke, I handed the Molly to Cray. Meanwhile, I made my way on the dance floor to find his boy toy. The only reason I was even doing this shit was because I owed him money. Had it not been for that I wouldn't be going nowhere near this fag.

Eventually, I made my way through the droves of women. A barrage of scents hit my nose as I made my way through crowd. Everything from Chanel no. 9 to that cheap cucumber shit from Bodyworks hit my nose.

Finally, I landed on that Sisqo lookin' nigga. He was leaning against the wall, standing on his hip like a woman as he scrolled through his phone. I prayed that no one caught me even talkin' to this nigga in the cut.

"Aye," I spat when I came over to him. Looking over my shoulders, I handed him the baggy when the coast was clear.

"I was hoping Von was gonna come. I ain't want him to send one of his worker bees."

"I don't work for him." I shook my head in disgust.

"Whatever. I guess he ain't wanna come cuz he with some fish tonight," he said while rolling his eyes with his lips pursed.

"I'm out," I spat.

"You finer than your daddy," he hollered at me as I stepped away. Apart of me wanted to turn around and throw my fist in his mouth but I decided to keep it moving. He wasn't worth it. As soon as I was done paying back Rayvon, I was done with that bullshit. No more gambling and definitely no more drugs. I just wanted to get money the most simplest way possible.

"Thanks for getting that for me," Cray said when I returned to the VIP section.

"You welcome. Y'all havin' fun?"

"Hell yea. This spot is nice. The bitches are bad. Shit I just got my assistant to book me a room. Finna have an orgy with a few of these bitches. Popped a Molly and a Viagra to keep up with all of them. You wanna roll so you can get in on this?" he asked looking over at the beautiful women.

They were all dancing with one another, looking fine as hell. All skin tones. Various hairstyles. Different body builds.

"I'm gonna have to pass," I replied. I was on a mission. The only woman I was kicking it with tonight was the one that could help me get some money. Those thots that Cray was about to fuck, would cost him money.

Around 1am, I decided that it was time to head out. My partner could finish closing the club since I was there for the opening. Besides, I got all the celebrities in that bitch which in turn brought all the bitches. After taking pics and posing with as many people as possible, I quietly dipped out so that I could meet Katya back at my spot.

When I got home, I walked through my spot to make sure that everything was clean. I didn't want her coming in here to a mess. In my personal stash I had Molly, Xanax, coke, weed and liquor. A lot of us on the scene kept that shit for the thots we messed with. A lot of them liked getting high.

The only thing I really fucked with was weed and liquor. On occasion, I'd party with some coke but everything else was too much for me. But I knew that when people were consistently under the influence, it made them make decisions they wouldn't normally make. And that's exactly where I wanted Katya. I needed her under my spell. Under my influence. And she seemed vulnerable enough to fall for it.

CHAPTER 10

Katya

Time moved slowly as I tried to keep myself awake in anticipation for Camden's call. I even drank a Red Bull so that I wouldn't fall asleep. Still dressed in my leopard jumpsuit, I paced the halls of my mansion while contemplating what I was doing. There was something about Camden that turned me on. And then to know that he also wanted to take care of his father, further made me want meet with him.

But then the little voice in my head started shouting as loud as possible. "You know this is wrong girl."

However, 1:00am, my husband was still not home. He rarely stayed out all night like this. He did most of his dirt while he was on the road traveling for "business." It was peculiar for him to still be out this late on a Saturday night.

Just the thought of him fucking someone else again after he'd given me that STD pissed me off. We had just gone through a situation yet he's out here slinging his dick around again. This nigga couldn't even be faithful for two weeks.

The more I thought about it, the more pissed I became. I began to anticipate Camden's call. I prayed he wasn't trying to play me. Getting back at Greer through fucking his son, delighted me. Sparks of joy shot through my clit at the thought of finally fucking someone in retaliation.

Up until this point, I'd been the good wife. I've never cheated on him even after the years of emotional abuse. Even when he told me he didn't want to have any more children. I stayed with him through it all. And he still hasn't started to respect me.

As my thoughts increased, my chest tightened. Sweat kissed the palms of my hands as my stomach rumbled. The walls of the mansion began to close in on me. Anger swept through my body like a forest fire. I hated Greer. And nothing would make me happier than standing over his casket while smirking.

Whether Camden called me or not, I was going to become a damn widow. I was smart enough to plot Greer's death on my own. And it wasn't just about the money. He was a damn demon. He walked around like he was God's gift to women. And I couldn't take it anymore.

As the wheels in my head churned, I finally got a text from Camden.

"Hey, I got caught up at the club. Sorry about making you wait. If you want, you can still come through. If not we can link another day."

"Send me the address. I'm on my way," I replied while scooping up my purse and rushing out the front door.

If I hadn't gotten out of that house, I probably would've set the place on fire. Tears poured down my cheeks as I drove to

Camden's condo. It was damn near 2am and Greer still wasn't home. He probably wouldn't even notice that I was missing once he gets back. Bitch.

Finally, I arrived at Camden's home. I checked the mirror to make sure that I hadn't cried mascara down my face. Thank God I invested in good 24-hour mascara because my lashes were still intact. Despite the tears, my make-up still looked perfect. Courtesy of high end products.

I took a deep breath and headed toward Camden's door. He quickly buzzed me up. My heart rate as I reached his door.

You can turn back at any time, Katya. That little angel on my shoulder spoke to me meanwhile the devil on the other disagreed.

Fuck the shit out of him.

Torn between two decisions, my body still led me to his door. I took a deep breath, allowing the oxygen to permeate every cell in my body while I waited for him to open.

"Come in," he spoke when he opened the door.

Hesitantly, I made my way across his threshold. He had a nice place. Minimalistic with a touch of swag. I can't lie, I was impressed.

"I ain't get to tell you how damn good you looked tonight," he commented as he closed the door behind me.

"All those other half naked chicks at the club had your attention instead," I laughed nervously.

"Nah, I was there to work. I wasn't there to look at no one else. You wanna smoke? Coke? Molly?" he offered as he swaggered over to his pristine kitchen. It was probably immaculate because he never cooked. He probably always ate out.

"Do you have any more Xanax? I'm more in to relaxing?"

"I got percs," he offered instead.

Fuck it, I thought to myself.

"Sure. What do you have to drink?" I asked. I knew that I needed something to help me build up my nerve.

"Wine."

"All I have is Moscato."

"That's fine."

Once he was finished pouring me a glass he came and sat next to me on the sofa. In his hand was a tumbler of a dark brown elixir.

"I guess I can't say you're trying to get me drunk. What you have is much stronger."

"Ha! Yeah. It's been a long night. I didn't drink at the club since I was on the job. I deserve this D'usse."

"I wanted to talk to you about what I said to you at Greer's birthday party..."

"About him cheating?"

"Yeah. I just feel so stuck and..."

"You want out?" he asked completing my sentence.

"Yes. But if I leave, I'll get nothing and honestly I want him to pay for what he's done to me."

He took a swig of his drink before placing it back down on the table. "That nigga is foul. He won't help his own son out. He treats his wife like shit. Honestly, he'd be better off dead than alive."

Camden turned and looked at me, his dark deep eyes burning into my soul. He was thinking the exact same thing that I was. I leaned back into the sofa and brought the glass of wine to my lips. As the sweet liquid washed down my throat, I felt relieved because he felt the same way that I did.

"I agree."

"I don't even want that much money. Just a million," he said.

"That's all? I'm willing to give you half."

"I'm not greedy. I do intend on making my own way in this world. I got plans. I just need some startup capital. See them white boys, their pops would loan them the money. But my father. Nah. He so damn petty."

"Yes the hell he is," I said as the pills and wine begin to take effect.

Camden had a serious strong aura about him. He had a similar presence to his father. Masculine and potent. Camden always seemed like the strong and silent type. I looked at his chiseled jaw as he pulled the drink to his mouth.

"How do we do this?" I asked.

His sensual tongue licked his bottom lip before he tucked it underneath his teeth in. "We gotta plan it. You live with him so you know all about his comings and goings. Once we get a clear picture of his schedule we can really plot."

"I don't really know when he's coming or going. For instance, I don't know where the hell he is tonight."

"Wait, he wasn't at home when you left?"

"Nope. That's what pissed me off and put fire under my ass to leave," I replied. The alcohol was making its way through my body. My chest felt warm and tight. My tongue was getting loose. I prayed I didn't spill the truth about the STD that Greer had given me. I was cured and I didn't want Camden judging me.

"I'm glad you came. Fuck that nigga. You can do better than him anyway," he spoke before swallowing the rest of his drink.

"Whatever we do, I'm not going to jail over this nigga. We have to make sure that our plan is airtight."

"It will be," he said before leaning over and looking at me. "I don't wanna go to prison either. I got you." His hand grazed my thigh. I placed my hand on top of his.

"If we do this, I have to be able to trust you. Are you messing with anyone right now?" I asked him. He could have a dirty dick like his father

"Nah, me and my girl just broke up. I'm all about my paper right now. And you."

"You got condoms?" I asked. I wasn't a damn fool. I would never be caught in that situation that Greer put me in. And even thought I knew it was wrong, I just wanted someone to want me for me.

I wanted Greer to hurt worse than I did. The moment before he dies, I want him to know that I was fucking his son. .

"Of course," Camden replied as he leaned forward and kissed me. Our lips touching, sent a signal to my pussy to moisten instantly.

I'd forgotten what it was like to be kissed. Greer never kissed me these days. There was no foreplay. He would just strip me naked and climb on top of me. I might as well had been a Fleshlight to him.

Camden rubbed his nose against mine, as he held my face closely. "He don't know what the fuck he has at home," he said to me before slipping his tongue between my lips.

Our tongues became acquainted as my body succumbed to his pleasure. Something about this moment being forbidden made me more excited. Wetness drained from me as we made out like a pair of teenagers on his sofa.

"Take that shit off," he said while looking me up and down as if he were ready to devour me.

Without hesitation, I stood to my feet and maneuvered out of the jumpsuit. I must have taken too long for him, because he jumped, dick poking through his jeans and helped me get out of the catsuit.

While I stood there in my black lacy bra and thong, he got down on his knees to admire my body. "Damn, I'm about to fuck you up," he growled as his hands traced my curves.

Nervously, I bit my bottom lip as he continued to caress me. I couldn't remember the last time someone stopped to appreciate the way that I looked. There was a part of me that was uncomfortable, but then there was another part of me that was in ecstasy. The percs and wine were allowing me to keep my guard down as his tongue trailed down my belly.

Ferociously he snatched my panties down and sat me back on his sofa. My eyes gazed at his strong arms. Veins bulged as his muscles flexed. He was in much better shape than Greer because of his age. His cocoa skin had a sheen underneath the dim lights that made me want to drag my skin over it.

Still planted on his knees, he draped my legs over his shoulders like a cape. He was coming to save my pussy. Once again, I couldn't remember the last time someone ate me out. Greer stopped going down on me a while ago. He would always say he didn't feel like it but expected me to suck his dick.

Camden trailed his nose across my clit before teasing me with his kisses. His lips danced across my inner thighs, making my sweet cave beg him to enter or lick her. Quivering under his touch, he picked up the ante. Suckling right by my lips, he ignored that pussy was pulsating in sweet desire for him to lick her.

"Tell me how bad you want it," he commanded while looking up at me. His bedroom eyes, burned into my soul.

"Kiss it..." I moaned, damn near squirming in agony.

"Kiss what?" he sensually asked before his lips met with my thigh again.

"Kiss my pussy..." I cried.

A sly grin played across his face as he dove in. His tongue began to dance over my clit causing me to flood. My legs shook against his shoulders as he pulled me in closer.

His hurricane tongue whirled and flicked, pulsating stronger than any vibrator I've ever known. To add to the intense pleasure, he slipped his fingers in my tight slit. Massaging my g-spot, he continued to suckle on my clit. Slurping sounds filled the air, mixing with my moans of pleasure.

Before I knew it my body convulsed against the sofa and I began to cum. "CAMDEN!" I hollered in pleasure as I released all my pent up energy.

I never came with Greer anymore. My organs were regulated to my vibrator. But this was different. This was the strongest orgasm I'd ever had in my life.

"I could drink you all night long," Camden whispered while still kissing sensitive clit. I pushed his head back away for reprieve.

Laughing, he said, "I ain't done with you yet."

He got up from his knees then helped me off of the sofa. My knees wobbled as I tried to gain my composure.

"Walk to the back. I wanna see that ass move." He nudged forward.

Doing as he said, I sauntered away. The orgasm, the liquor and the percs made me feel as if I were floating on a cloud.

When I reached his room, I noticed how neat it was. A large king bed sat in the center with a black comforter over it. Large plush pillows sat at the top while a gray throw was folded at the bottom.

"Get on all fours," he commanded.

Doing as he said, I hopped on the bed and assumed the position. I pressed my chest to the mattress while I arched my ass to the heavens. I watched as he made his way to the nightstand where he pulled out a XL Magnum.

With his eyes staring at me, he quickly undressed, revealing his bulging muscles. His smooth brown skin was covered in tattoos. When I looked down at his dick, I did a little praise dance inside. He had inches and girth. His dick was even bigger than his father's. And to top it off, he had a nice curve to it.

Slowly he made his way behind me and got on the bed. His hands glided all over my body as he took the tip of his dick and stroked my clit.

"Condom." I demanded.

"I got you," he replied. I could hear him unwrap the rubber. He paused to slide the condom down his shaft before rubbing against me against.

"Fuck me," I commanded.

Without notice, he slid his dick inside of me. The sensation of my walls conforming to his large dick, made tears form in my eyes. "Shit..." I moaned.

"I know, it's different," he teased as he moves slowly to open me up. My walls were forgiving. On impact they grew wet as he pushed in and out of me. That curve led him to hitting my throbbing g-spot at the perfect angle.

Every time the two collided, I quivered and clutched his sheets even harder. The back shots grew stronger as he pumped in and out of me ferociously.

"Fuck!" I screamed unable to hold myself up anymore. My body collapsed onto the bed while he held my ass steady, grinding inside me.

"Damn, Katya. This some good pussy," he grunted as his hips swirled in and out of me.

"Hmmmm." No words would form out of my mouth. I had to bite down on the sheets as his dick dug deeper and deeper. He bypassed my guts and went straight to my heart.

The energy swelled within me again. Starting at my g-spot and expanding throughout my entire body. "Shit!"

He placed his hand at the back on my neck and drilled into me even deeper to get that orgasm out. I exploded into a million pieces. That fiery energy shot through my body. Every limb shook. Every cell pulsated.

"Yeah that's right. Cum on this dick," Camden cockily said.

Eventually he busted his nut before sliding out of me and landing next to me. Drenched in sweat, I laid on my belly while the feeling swirled around my body. The air was thick with pheromones, my perfume and his cologne. He reached over and slapped my ass, watching it ripple and jiggle.

I wish I could say I felt some guilt or shame. But instead, I was thinking about how I good it would be next time.

"Get on top," he demanded after taking off the condom and putting on the new one. He had the type of dick that could bust and keep going. Those days for Greer were over. Well, who knew what he did with the bitches he slept with.

"I need a second," I laughed.

"Fuck that. Ride me Katya," he demanded with sincerity in his eyes.

Not wanting the night to be over, I did just that. I mounted him. With all the strength and energy I could muster, I grinded on his dick.

We went a couple more rounds. That nigga was the Energizer Bunny. But eventually he tired and passed out after three nuts.

While he slept, I got dressed in my jumpsuit and took my ass home. As my car glided through the bare streets, the sun began to its daily entrance. A devilish smile spread across my face. Greer was probably going to be heated with me coming in this early in the morning.

The thought of seeing him sweat and hurt, made me laugh. I've always wanted to know what it was like to waltz in the house after a long night of cheating just to see that dumb look on his face. The same dumb look I make.

The closer I got to the house, the more excited I became at seeing his reaction. I felt no guilt or shame for what I'd done. In fact I was proud of myself for standing up to myself.

With that pride, I arrived home, only for egg to be smashed on my face.

Greer still wasn't home.

CHAPTER 11

C amden

It was the high noon sun, pushing through my blinds that finally lured me out of my sleep. Groggy, I finally got my tired body out of the bed. Katya was gone. The space where she laid was rustled and the pillows were on the floor.

"Shit..." I grunted to myself. A slight headache stretched across my forehead. Dehydration had set in. Busting three nuts back to back and drinking alcohol will drain a nigga.

When I stood to my feet, I realized I was still naked. Something I never do. I always sleep in shorts, even if I fucked afterwards.

But there was something about Katya. I wasn't expecting for it to be like that. I just thought that we would fuck. I'd get in her head so that she would be more willing to go along with my plan. However, she did something to me.

As soon as I saw her naked body, I got excited. I saw bad bitches on a daily. Beautiful women with big titties and fat asses threw themselves at me often but there was something about Katya. She had this sensual energy about her. If I could, I would've stayed in her pussy all night.

Memories were on replay as I made my way to the shower to wake myself up. Thoughts of her bouncing on my ass intruded my mind while the cold water washed over my body. She did this thing where she spun while my dick was still up in her. I ain't never seen a bitch who could do some shit like that.

What the fuck was my father thinking? He had all of that at home. A fine ass woman, who cooked, took care of the house and stayed out of public drama. She was a rarity when it came to women in this industry.

My pops was dumb for how he treated her. After last night, it made me want to take my father out even more. Not just for my sake but for hers too.

After I finished in the shower, I made my way into the kitchen to rehydrate. I passed my sofa and looked over it at. Another memory popped in my head. Her sugary sweet pussy on my lips made my dick get hard.

I needed to have her again. I couldn't stop thinking about her. This was weird for me. No other bitch had every captured me like that.

It's crazy because through the years, I never looked at her like that. Sure, I acknowledged that she was fine. It was hard not to notice. She was the ex-video girl. But I always kept my distance.

However, the older I got, I started to noticed her even more. She'd pop up on my explore feed on Instagram. Or I'd see her out on the scene with her crew but I hadn't really noticed her. Not until that night at my father's party.

A part of it was because of how my mother felt about her. Even though my pops was divorced from my mother when he met Katya, she was always bitter about it. He went out and got a younger woman to replace her. That's how she thought.

When I was a kid, I didn't know any better. But as a grown ass man, when you're broken up with someone all bets are off. You can be with whoever the fuck you wanna be with.

Just as I finished my water, I heard a knock on my door. I hated when other residents in the condo let people inside without making them get buzzed in first.

In a huff, I marched to the front door. I was annoyed that someone would come over here without calling first. My fist instincts told me that it was probably Rayvon but we'd just spoken last night. I know that nigga wouldn't be pressing me the next day.

Dressed in only my gray sweats, I looked through the peephole to find that it was Naija.

"Wsup?" I asked when I opened the door.

"Can I come in?" she asked with her hand on her hip. She was only about three months so she wasn't fully showing yet.

"Yeah," I replied before walking away from the door.

"I need to talk to you." She closed the door behind her and made her way into the condo.

As she adjusted her purse on her shoulder, she sank into my sofa, right in the spot where I ravaged Katya.

"Talk."

"Why are you being so cold to me?" she asked.

"Listen, you walked away. You broke up with me. As far as I'm concerned we ain't got shit to talk about it if ain't about the baby," I said while standing away from her .

In comparison to Katya, Naija ain't have nothing on her. Naija was cute but Katya was a goddess. I couldn't believe how bad Katya had my head fucked up.

After you get some pussy from a woman like Katya, you could never go back to a bitch like Naija. As soon as Naija got on top, she complained about her knees hurting. She couldn't sit all the way on the dick. Even from the back, she did that thing that cats do.

Meanwhile, Katya took all of my inches like a pro. I was even impressed at how she kept throwing it back for me to catch it.

"Did you hear what I said?" Naija asked, interrupting my thoughts.

"Nah, my bad. What did you say?"

"I said, my mother is kicking me out. She gave me a month. I don't have anywhere else to go. Can I move back in with you?" she asked me.

It was like hearing a record skip. My initial reaction was "fuck no." But I bit my tongue in search for a gentler response.

"Naija, I don't want us to get confused about what it is between us. You living here isn't gonna be a good idea. But I would never want to you be homeless. Especially not with my seed. So I'ma get the bread so you can get your own place," I replied.

I wasn't sure how I was going to pull that off. Especially with me owing Rayvon and still taking care of my bills. And now that I was plotting with Katya, I definitely didn't want Naija in my space.

"You really hate me that much? I can't even live with you? We've only been broken up for a few weeks," she looked up at me as if she were going to cry.

"I don't hate you, Naija. I'm single now and I wanna stay that way. I don't want you in my space again. Especially not while I'm working. I got 7 months to make shit pop for this baby. I'm gon' always take care of you. So give me a month. If I can't get the bread by the time you mother puts you out, you can stay here. Why she puttin' you out anyway?" I asked.

"We got into it... It got bad. I just can't be in a stressful environment while I'm pregnant."

"I agree. I'll work it out," I replied. My responsibilities began to weigh on me like a ton of bricks. My shoulders felt heavy but I was determined to keep my head up. I was going to find a way out of this shit. And once I get that cash from my father, my life would be smooth sailing.

"I'll be back, I gotta pee."

"Aight," I replied before walking over to my coffee table. I pulled out a Dutch and my grinder. The tension in my body made me crave some Kush. It would help me think while I plotted out my father's death. I knew that I wouldn't get any money from his estate in a month so I needed to figure out another way to get money for Naija.

As soon as I sparked the joint, I heard Naija holler, "CAMDEN!"

"What?" I asked as I placed the weed down. I rushed to the bathroom to see what had happened. She didn't sound hurt. Instead she sounded angry.

When I finally arrived to the bathroom, I could see exactly why she was angry. In between her fingers she held a used condom that I had thrown in the trash last night. My face scrunched at how disgusting it was of her to pick it up.

"Who is she?" Naija asked. Semen dripped from the rubber onto the ground.

"Yo, put that shit in the trash. It's leaking everywhere."

"I don't give a fuck! Who is she!?" she asked me again before throwing used condom at my face, but I dodged it with the quickness.

"Aight, time for you to go."

"Who the fuck is the bitch that you're fucking!? Huh? Who is she? That's why you don't want me to move in with you?!"

"Calm down Naija. My neighbors are gonna be able to hear you."

"No nigga! You about to have me homeless so you can fuck randoms? It's been three weeks and you already bussin' down thots?!" she hollered even louder.

The minor headache I had earlier had turned into full blown migraine. Rather than argue with this crazy girl, I walked away from the bathroom. Shit could turn ugly quickly, and I wanted to avoid that drama.

"Fuck you nigga!" she screamed as she marched behind me.

"You broke any damn way. That's what I get for fuckin' a broke nigga. The bitch probably ugly to be fuckin' with you.

What kinda pussy can you pull? You ain't got no bread!" she screamed. It was another side of her, that I had never seen before.

"I ain't need bread." I laughed while grabbing my dick.

"Your dick ain't all that."

"You can't even take dick, so how you know. Teeth scraping all against it when you give me head. Can't ride for shit. Stay running from the dick," I replied while thinking about just how good Katya was. It was the most inappropriate time to be thinking of her.

However, Naija's rage brought me back down to Earth. What I said had incited her to make her way into my kitchen. Quickly she threw open the cabinets and began to toss my dishes on the ground.

"Yo, what the fuck is your problem?" I asked.

"Fuck you nigga!" she screamed as she continued to break dishes.

"Yo Naija, calm down. You're gonna get the cops called."

But she didn't let up. She continued with the racket until I grabbed her by her arms and pulled her out of the kitchen.

"Get your hands off of me, bitch!"

"NAIJA STOP!" I asked of her. Whatever semblance of a high that I felt had crashed. My head was pounding and I was 100% sober.

She broke away from my clutch and slapped me. These pregnancy hormones had her acting like a banshee. "Yo get the fuck out!" I barked at her.

"You ain't shit!" She screamed.

"I don't care if your mother throws you out on to the streets in a cardboard box," I said while grabbing her and opening the door.

Just as I touched the doorknob I heard a loud bang. Judging from the sound of the knock, I already knew who it was. The damn police.

"POLICE! Is everything okay?"

"NO!!!" Naija screamed. Apart of me wanted to punch that bitch in her mouth but I was going to jail already.

I sighed and opened the door. Eventually I was placed in handcuffs and seated in the back of a squad car.

CHAPTER 12

Katya

Hazily, I laid in the bed that I shared with Greer. This place had become my prison cot. And even after he'd been gone all day it was still void of him. I extended my arm across where he would normally lay, and it felt cold and barren.

The blackout shades were drawn tightly, so there wasn't a slither of sunlight piercing the room. Without any knowledge of what time it was, I pulled my body out of the bed. My inner thighs and pussy was sore from the pounding I took last night.

Flashes of Camden fucking me, entered my mind. He was damn good. I couldn't lie. He was better than any lover I'd ever had. He had a way with his tongue and hands that some bitches would pay for. I'd never came so much in one night.

Thirsty and sore, I wandered over to the blinds and drew them back. Sunlight came gushing in, washing all over my face and body. I'd slept naked because I was too tired to dig for a night gown when I came home early morning.

In fact the disappointment of not seeing Greer in the house, drove me straight to the liquor cabinet. I'd taken two shots of gin before crashing in our unloving bed. I knew that my drinking was getting bad when I took shots at 6am. But that's what my husband was driving me to. Fucking his son and drinking.

Still exhausted, I reached for my phone to check the time. It was after 2:00. Where in the fuck was he? Was he that disrespectful to be out with another bitch all night and day? This was well over the line. He crossed it when he gave me that damn STD. And now this.

Pissed, I began to call him. He was driving me up a wall with his antics. It was so reckless of him to be out like this and not even bother to contact me. I threw on some black yoga pants a tank top before leaving our wretched bedroom.

Stomping through the mansion, I phoned him back to back. But it just kept ringing. Eventually, I was blocked. I was going straight to voicemail.

"Wow!" I blurted out loud.

This nigga hated me. I'd done nothing to him. But I was going to. I was going to kill him. I was going to murder him my damn self. I wanted to pull the trigger or light the match. I deserved to have that power after what he's done to me.

My chest tightened while my heart punched through my chest like a heavy weight champ. My breathing became shallow. I was on the brink of a full blown panic attack. Beads of sweat formed at my forehead as tears leaked from my eyes. I didn't deserve this.

Outraged, I rushed to my Xanax collection and took two pills calm me down. When it didn't work instantaneously, I rushed to back to my bottle of gin. Two shots were all it took. Once the Xanax and the liquor took over, I began to calm down

Inhaling deeply, I walked up to my private room, where I crashed on the chaise lounge chair. Tears seeped down my face out of sadness. But then I remembered last night. I remembered the way that Camden tongued my pussy down. I remembered his stroke.

I wanted him again. He made me feel better and right now, I felt like shit. Just the feel of his dick could take my pain away.

I then tried to call him, but he didn't answer. Perhaps he was still knocked out from last night. Rolling my eyes, I decided to call up Markisa. I wanted to see if she were down to go shopping.

"Hey girl. BOYS SHUT THE HELL UP!" she yelled her twins. "Sorry about that," she redirected her attention to me.

"Are you busy right now?"

"No. We just got in from karate. It's Shawn's turn to deal with them. Mama needs a mimosa right about now," she laughed. I could hear the exhaustion in her voice.

"Do you wanna go shopping. Everything on me. We can run up a few of Greer's credit cards. I can def get you a mimosa. Shit bottomless if you want," I offered.

"What the hell he do now?"

"I don't even want to get into it. Just know that I need some retail therapy," I replied.

"Do you want me to drive? After riding in my 'experience' I just doesn't feel right driving in anything else right now," she spoke. I was thoroughly annoyed by her bourgeoisie attitude and I was tired of hearing about the damn 'experience.' But at this point I didn't want to be alone. I'd have to deal with her ridiculousness for now.

"You can come scoop me."

"I'll be there soon," she said before hanging up on me.

Quickly, I hopped in the shower. My body still felt light after the Xanax and the gin. It felt even nice as the hot water rushed over my skin, washing last night's sin down the drain. Thoughts of Camden rushed my mind.

I remembered how he grabbed the back of my neck with passion as his dick opened me wide. Chills ran over my body. I couldn't wait to feel him inside of me again. I just wished that Greer was home when I got there. I would've walked through confident.

He would've wondered where I'd been. I know he would've been pressing me to tell him. However, I'd keep my mouth shut. Never revealing the truth. I'd lavish in my dirty secret. I been fucking your son. But no.

This nigga didn't come home. He'd been out for almost 24 hours. Instead, I was home looking like a fool. I couldn't wait to make him pay for this shit.

After my hot shower, I got dressed. Keeping it simple, I wore a pair of black jeans with slits in the knees. A Gucci sweatshirt and a pair of Gucci sneakers. I swept my blonde bob into a top knot and accompanied the updo with a pair of large gold hoops. A bright red lip adorned my mouth to complete the simple look.

When I was done, I popped another Xanax and took two more shots of the gin. By the time I was inebriated, Markisa was calling me to come outside.

Even though I was tipsy, I was able to walk in a straight line and hold myself together. And thankfully, you couldn't smell the gin on my breath. I'd popped a mint in my mouth.

"Hey! You look cute. I swear ever since you showed up to that brunch lookin' a mess I been worried about you. But you've definitely stepped up your game these last few outings," she laughed while pulling off.

"Yeah, I guess." I was too lifted to hear what she was saying. I just wanted to ride out. I lowered the windows and stuck my arm outside of the vehicle to let the air kiss my fingertips. I couldn't wait for Greer to die. Nothing would bring me more joy.

Eventually, we arrived at the Lenox and we went crazy. First we hit up the Louis Vuitton store.

"Is it too much if I ask you to get me a luggage set?" Markisa asked jokingly. Each piece cost somewhere between $2000 and $5000.

"If that's what you want." I shrugged, still calm from my cocktail.

"You are not serious."

"As a heart attack," I stated flatly.

"Damn what did Greer do."

"Doesn't matter. Get what you want," I said while laughing.

"If you say so..." Markisa looked at me skeptically but that didn't stop her from getting the salesclerk to gather her luggage sat.

Because we were spending so much money, they popped open a bottle of Crystal. Not that I needed it, but I was definitely excited to have more to drink.

After two glasses of champagne and $25,000 on my husband's card, we headed out. We had the clerks at Louis Vuitton fill her 'experience' up with her goodies so that we could keep shopping. There was no way we could keep going while carrying all that luggage.

I laughed at the irony.

As we stepped into Saks, Markisa pulled me to the side. "Girl I feel bad."

"Why?"

"Spending all of Greer's money like that."

"Fuck him," my words slurred as I staggered into the department store.

"Wait a minute, Katya."

"What?" I asked when I turned around.

"We only had two glasses of champagne. Why are you drunk?" she asked, looking me up and down.

I steadied myself on my two feet and looked at her but I was seeing double. The Xanax, gin and champagne were hitting hard.

"I'm not drunk. The champagne was just a little strong. I'm fine," I spoke slowly to be careful not to slur my words again.

"I knew I shouldn't have been encouraging this. I thought you had your drinking under control. I didn't think it was a problem anymore," Markisa said referring to a few years ago. I'd gone through rehab for coke. They told me not to drink but I never had a problem with alcohol. I had a problem with cocaine.

"I'm fine. I don't even drink like that." I lied. It had been an everyday occurrence for me since I found out about the STD.

"Listen, we're going to go. I'm giving you the money back for that luggage too."

"What? No. You're being dramatic, Markisa."

"No I'm not. Let's just go. We can go to my house and sit in the hot tub and just talk. You can tell me what's going on between you and Greer. I'm your friend. I know I joke a lot but you can confide in me," she said while pulling me in and walking me away from Saks.

Embarrassment flooded my body as we made our way back to her car. My drinking was getting out of control but it was helping me deal with the crumbling of my marriage. And even though Markisa and I were close, I didn't want to talk to her about what was going on with me and Greer. I was tired of the world knowing our business. I just wanted to keep the pain to myself.

As we walked through the mall, she whipped out her phone to check her text messages. "Oh my God!" she said while stopping dead in her tracks. She covered her mouth with her hand and shook her head.

"Jordyn just texted me..."

"Okay...

"I understand why you didn't want to tell me what's going on between you and Greer. You must be so heartbroken. Let's just go to my home."

"What are you talking about?" I asked as the mall began to spin.

"This..." she said while handing me her phone.

When I read what Jordyn texted her, I felt as if the rug had been pulled from underneath me. As my knees buckled, my stomach dropped to my chest. It was finally clear why my husband hadn't been home in a day.

CHAPTER 13

Camden

With my back leaned against the cool cinder blocks, I kept my eyes closed. My mother was going to be here at any moment to bail me out. I used my one free call on her. Anger rattled my nerves as I tried to keep calm in that holding cell.

If I'd known I was going to be arrested for assault against Naija, I would've actually assaulted the bitch. She deserved a quick slap across the face for how she acted at my place. Stupid bitch. Now I'm in here on an assault charge.

Regret ran through my mind. I should've never let her in my condo. I should've never busted a nut in her. She wasn't worth it. The pussy definitely wasn't worth this drama.

As my mind churned, thinking about where I went wrong, I thought about Katya. Thoughts of her made me relax even though I was in one of the most uncomfortable positions. The memory of her bouncing on my dick flooded my mind and I couldn't wait to feel her again.

The more time I spent away from her, the more obsessed with her I became. I wanted her with me all the time. But I had to work this shit out with Naija. Fuck! Now that I've been arrested, she's going to find out all about Naija.

I already know that the blogs are going to be talking about me getting arrested for abusing her. Shit ain't even true. But that bitch was out of luck now. She wouldn't get a red cent out me. Any money will have to be directly for the baby. I was going to take care of her but not anymore. I was going to make sure I made it hard for her in court too.

"Song!" A guard shouted my last name.

Finally, my mother had arrived.

Quickly, I hopped up and made my way to the door of the cell.

"Knucklehead out here beatin' on your woman. You and ya daddy some trash," the guard said while shaking his head.

I was never going to be able to live this down. Everywhere I go, people were going to think that I was a woman beater.

Frustrated, I eventually met my mother in the front. It broke my heart to see the disappointed look on her face.

"Ma..."

"Boy I don't even wanna hear it," she said while shaking her head and walking out the door.

For the remainder of the car ride, she kept silent. Her hands gripped the wheel as she quickened down the road. I felt bad that she even had to come get me from jail over this bullshit.

"I'll talk to you later," she said when we arrived at my condo.

"Aight. Thanks."

As soon as I closed the door, she sped away. I really wanted to repay Naija for this shit but I had to move on. There were bigger fish to fry. Finally, I made it back in my apartment.

My shit was a wreck because of Naija's crazy ass. Broken glass and ceramic littered my floor. Now, I had to be the one to clean this mess up.

While I swept up my broken dishes, I got a call from my homeboy Marco.

"What you up to?" he asked when I answered the phone.

"Chillin'. I had a rough day."

"Aight, I gotta talk to you about some shit. I'ma bring a bottle."

"Cool, come through."

As soon as we got off the phone I received another call. This time it was from Cray.

"What up?" I answered still flustered after having to sweep up my shit.

"Bruh, what's going on with you?"

"What you mean?"

"Word is traveling about you getting arrested for beating your baby mother," he spoke.

"It's a misunderstanding. It's a long ass story and I don't feel like getting into it right now."

"Look, we homeboys. We been cool since we were younger but this shit ain't a good look. My manager is trying to take my brand to the next level. I'm tryna get that family money.

You feel me? Lebron James. Steph Curry. I can't be hanging with no woman beater."

"I'm not a woman beater. She lied," I stated firmly. My jaw clinched as I listened to him. That bitch Naija really fucked me over because now the only thing people are going to see when they look at me is that I'm a woman beater.

"Whatever it is. I gotta distance myself from you for a while. I'ma come through and get my whip," he said before hanging up.

Fury rushed over me as I tossed my phone to the sofa. Pissed that Naija had cost me my whip, I slammed my fist into the wall out of anger. When I retracted my hand, my knuckles were cracked and bleeding. This day was all kinds of fucked up.

Frustrated, I made my way to the kitchen and fished out a bottle of Cîroc. Since I'd been running low on funds, my refrigerator was bare. I had to drink that shit straight no chaser. As I knocked the liquor down my throat, my thoughts spun out of control.

Shit was piling up. I really needed some cash and I needed it fast. Plotting to kill my pops would take much longer than I had time for. But Katya and I needed this badly. We both needed to get rid of my father.

I prayed that Katya didn't find out about Naija. She would def stop fucking with me if she knew.

As the thoughts rushed me, I took another shot of Cîroc. Just as I placed the bottle back down, I heard my phone go off. It was Marco looking to be buzzed in.

"Sup," he greeted when he stepped through the door.

"This shit... I'm fucked right now," I replied as he closed the door behind him.

"Damn bruh. I got the weed. But what the fuck happened?" he asked.

He handed the bag and Backwood over to me. While I fixed my attention on rolling the weed, I told him all about what happened with Naija.

"Wait, she just came in here and started acting a fool?"

"Yep. Fuckin' hormones. Broke all my dishes and shit. Then my neighbors called the cops. They probably thought I was in here killing her. They show up and she does nothing to stop them from arresting me. Stupid bitch. How she expect to get any type of support if I got a record."

"True. This could def hurt your collaborations with the clubs."

"Cray already talkin' 'bout he gotta distance himself from me. This my homie from pre-k! He saying he can't fuck with me already. And he on his way to come get the whip."

"Wait, what?" Marco asked with his face screwed tightly.

"He called as soon as I stepped in this bitch from jail. He said he's trying to get that family money. And that he can't fuck with an abuser. I'm not even an abuser," I replied before lighting the Backwood.

I took a strong pull and inhaled the smoke all the way down in my lungs. Little by little the cells in my body began to relax. The tension in my shoulders melted as I eased into the couch. I watched as the dense smoke unfurled from lips, mixing in the atmosphere.

"Damn, I thought y'all was tight. He not even willing to support you? Have your back? Y'all been friends for forever."

"Exactly. That's what's fucking with me. Now, I don't have a car. Who knows when I'm gonna be able to make some money. Shit is just fucked up," I said while taking another pull.

When I tried to pass it to Marco he held up his hand and said, "nah, you need it more than I do. I might be able to help you out though..." he said while turning his gaze toward the ceiling.

Marco also did club promotion but on a much smaller scale. His main hustle were several smaller scams, robberies and smuggling illegal shit.

"Help me how?" I asked, looking at him sideways. I wasn't trying to sell drugs again. That shit was way too hot.

"Let me think about it. I know you ain't tryna move no weight. I'm not either. There's less risky ways to get paper."

As we sat there in silence, my phone rang again. This time it was Cray. Annoyed, I buzzed him up and let him.

"Hey," he said when he stepped in the condo. He looked to the right and noticed the hole in the wall. Shaking his head he sat in the chair across from Marco and I. "You ain't hit her?" he asked while looking back at the hole.

"Nope. I did that when I got home from jail," I replied while raising my bruised fist.

"What's going on? What's gotten into you?" he asked.

"Fuck you mean? The bitch came over here actin' a damn fool. Broke damn near all my dishes. The neighbors called the cops. I was the one dragged out of here in cuffs," I replied just as I finished off the blunt. I tossed the roach into an ash tray. I then dug in my pockets to fish out my keys.

Once Cray's key of the ring, I slid it on the coffee table. "There you go."

"Look, man. You my brother. But I gotta protect my legacy at all costs. I got a lot riding on my success. And I don't want any controversies. I'm starting this season. And this could land me all kinds of deals. You gon' always be my fam but for right now, we need to distance ourselves."

"Man whatever," I said as I leaned back in the sofa. Marco sat in silence as he listened to the awkward conversation.

"That's all you gotta say to me?"

"What the fuck else am I supposed to say?"

"I been looking out for you. But you gotta get your shit together bro. You gon' be 30 in two years. A baby mother and a car repossession. It's time you grow the fuck up."

"Just get the fuck up out my crib. I don't need no lectures from you," I said dismissing him.

Cray snatched the key off of the table and headed out of the door.

"This day can't get any worse," I said as I interlaced my fingers behind my head and looked up toward the ceiling.

"How much you think the jewelry he was wearing is worth?" Marco asked. I could see that his wheels were turning.

"Quarter of a million probably. Why?"

"Rob that nigga!" Marco smiled, showing off his fronts.

"What?"

"He on some petty shit by taking the car back. Cutting you off and shit. Rob that nigga. Resell that shit. I'll help you. We can split it 50/50."

I grew silent and took a deep breath. "Nah..."

"No? Why not? He's laced!"

"We won't rob him. We'll rob his moms. She got a crazy collection that he bought her. She live in the same neighborhood as my mother. You see his security is tight. Hers isn't. I know her shit very well. Robbing her will be low risk."

"Shit... you're really thinking. When you tryna pull this off?" Marco asked.

"A.S.A.P. Like next weekend. I can't survive another month without a cash flow," I replied.

"Cool. Let's iron out the details now."

For the rest of the evening we planned how to get this quick money. If Cray wanted to throw away our friendship. Then I was going to incinerate it. All bets were off. And his mother, Ms. Vanessa, was going to have to lose her precious jewels.

CHAPTER 14

K atya

My entire body was shaking as tears poured from my eyes. My heart pounded as if it were going to explode out of my chest and land on to Markisa' dashboard. The tension in my neck was so thick that I couldn't turn my head if I wanted to.

Together we sat in the parking garage while I tried to come to terms with the worst news I've ever heard. It was worse than when I found out that I had the STD. What had I done to be treated like this?

"Let's just go back to my place?" Markisa offered.

"Twins..." my lips opened. That was the first word, I'd said since I found out that one of my husband's side bitches just gave birth to twins. A boy and a girl.

"I know it's a lot to accept right now. Listen, we can go back to my house and drink a bottle of wine."

"TWINS! For years he's told me he didn't want any more children. I wanted kids! But no, I stuffed an IUD into my cervix to keep him happy. And he goes out and does this!? A boy and a girl by some ran through thot!" I broke down crying again.

Fucking his son wasn't even worse than this in my opinion. If I had a gun, I'd go shove the barrel into his forehead right now. I'd pull the trigger and laugh in my mugshot. Bitch. Both of them. She knew he was married, nasty skank.

Her name was Ashantay. She was a well-known groupie. She typically fucked with younger ballers but it was my old ass husband that knocked her up. Tears rained down my cheeks like it was hurricane season.

"Take me home," I said to Markisa.

"No. I don't think you should go there."

"TAKE ME TO MY HOME!" I shouted as I wiped the tears from my eyes.

"Okay. I'll stay with you tonight. Let me just call Shawn and tell him..."

"No. I need to be alone," I sobbed.

Nodding her head in defeat, she pulled out of the parking lot and took me back to my mansion of horrors.

"You sure you don't want me to come in with you?" Markisa asked when she finally pulled back in front of my home.

"I'm sure. I'm good," I replied as I marched into the house. He still wasn't there. He still hadn't called me. He had so little respect for my feelings that he was okay with me finding out on social media.

As soon as I got in, I grabbed the keys to the G Wagon. Once I was sure that Markisa had pulled off, I jumped out the car and made my way to the hospital. The social media chatter said that Ashantay was at Georgetown.

With my foot to the gas, I sped there ready to rip that bitch a part. My drunken buzz had settled and was replaced with rage forging fire through my veins. Killing something was the only thing on my mind.

I was barely conscious on the ride there. My anger was so vicious that I only saw red. I wasn't even sure how I arrived at the hospital in one piece. But I did.

I parked right in front of the emergency room without a care in the world. Fuck those ambulances. I had to go rip a bitch's stitches.

"Ma'am!" Someone hollered at me as I made my way through the ER and eventually to the elevator.

I'd visited many friends who'd given birth here. I knew exactly where the maternity ward was located. I was a woman on a mission. Tired of sitting by and letting my husband disrespect me, I wanted to take matters into my own hands.

"Security!" Someone yelled before I ran into the elevator.

Trembling from head to toe, I stood on the elevator anticipating beating this bitch as she laid in her hospital bed from recovering from the babies she wasn't supposed to have.

For years, I begged Greer for more children. He kept telling me he didn't want any more. That having a son was enough for him. And that he would be the best father for Zania but he didn't have any more to give.

The real truth is, he didn't want to have to pay child support if we divorced. But now he will have to pay it to some side bitch.

"Excuse me, who are you here to see?" A nurse asked me as stomped down the maternity ward.

Ignoring her, I continued, glancing at each door's name tag until I finally reached hers.

"Ma'am…" a nurse called out to me. Rather than turn around and acknowledge her, I barged into Ashantay's suite. She was asleep but guess who was right by her side.

"Katya? What are you doing here?" Greer asked when he stood up from his seat.

"I will fucking kill you!" I screamed as I raced past him and jumped to her bed.

"AHHH!" She screamed when I smashed into her c-section incision. I pulled at her abdomen with such joy in my heart. Her rotten womb carried those bastard seeds and I wanted to punish her. She wailed in pain while trying to kick me away but I got one good punch to her face, before Greer pulled me off of her.

"HELP PLEASE!" She hollered in agony. Blood poured from her incision making me laugh maniacally.

"I hope you get a staph infection bitch!" I hollered at her.

"What the fuck is wrong with you, Katya?!" Greer shook me. He dragged me out of her hospital room as she continued to cry in agony.

A sinister grin spread across my face. "What the fuck am I doing? What are you doing? You could've easily avoided this by telling me to my face! You lying piece of shit!" I hawked spit right into Greer's face.

"Bitch have you lost your mind!?" he asked, ready to slap me. But he regained his composure. We had a full audience standing around us. Several visitors were standing around while aiming their phones in our direction.

"No you have! First you give me a STD and now this! You dirty dick bitch. I hate you. I hope you die. I'd kill you right here if all these people weren't watching!" I screamed at him.

A chorale of whispers filled the air. I had just put our business on front street but I didn't care. I was deranged. I was completely out of my element and not myself at all. Every woman has a breaking point. And I was right at mine. Boiling over for the world to see. Sweat dripped from my frizzy edges as I stood there looking like a crazy.

I could still hear Ashantay screaming as nurses rushed to tend to her open wound. I could smell the anger bouncing from Greer's pores. He wanted to retaliate and it was killing him that he couldn't.

"You know you're going to prison you insane bitch," he grunted while looking past me. I could hear the steps of officers approaching us from behind.

"You better hope they keep me forever," I grinned.

As soon as I felt the officers get close, I placed my hands behind my back. I knew I was getting arrested and I didn't care because for once I stood up to myself.

Everything after that moment was a blur. Images of being hauled off in the police car smeared into the booking experience. Fingerprinting, the mugshot and my call to Markisa to get me a lawyer.

I wouldn't be able to see a judge for a hearing for two days. But I knew that I wasn't going to be kept here until the trial.

"Song," a guard called out to me.

I made my way to the door of the cell. She opened the small gate and passed me a blanket and a small pillow. It was about the size of those pillows that airlines give you in coach. The shit was completely pointless. There would be no comfort derived from that little thin thing.

"Thank you," I replied.

"You don't remember me do you?" she asked. I glanced up to analyze her face. She was chubby, with a sugar cookie complexion and a pair of dimples. Her braids were cornrowed in an up do.

"I'm sorry," I whispered.

"It's me Keisha Richardson. We went to high school together."

"Oh hey Keisha. It's been a rough ass day," I replied.

"Yeah I can see. You had a rough ass life," she said before walking away.

It was true. While I don't remember much about Keisha, I remembered that time period when I met her. As I hard as I tried to forget that moment in my life, I haven't been able to.

I settled on the cot and laid on the little pillow as I thought about everything that I'd been through. I grew up with an abusive alcoholic mother. Every day if she wasn't passed out drunk, she was going upside my head.

My father left her when I was just a baby. I've never met the man. As a matter of fact, I've never seen a picture of him. My mother told me that when he left she burned all of his belongings. She burned any proof that he was ever in our lives. She told me I was her child and to never ask her about my father.

Of course, I couldn't live like that. Children are curious. Therefore, I frequently asked her about my father. Usually she would tell me something like he died. But if she were drunk, she would slap me for asking.

The abuse got worse the older I got. If I were talking to my friends on the phone and she felt like I shouldn't be, she would go into a rage. If I didn't wash dishes the way she liked, I she would beat me. If the sky was gray and she really wanted a sunny day, she would beat me.

Eventually, I found peace and solace in my boyfriend. A nigga who was too old to be dating a 16 year old. His name was Ricky. A small time drug dealer that was 21 years old when we started fucking. When I got pregnant, he ghosted because he was afraid to go to prison.

I was too afraid to tell anyone I was pregnant but eventually my mother figured it out. She threatened me to get an abortion, but I didn't. Instead I had Zania at 16. Then a miracle happened right after Zania was born.

My mother slammed her car into a phone pole and died. It occurred two months shy of my 18th birthday. I say it was a miracle because she had a small insurance policy. It was only $25,000 but it was enough to move Zania and I to Atlanta from Virginia. When I was in ATL I started doing music videos to stay afloat. Eventually, I met Greer who retired from the league.

Growing up with low self-esteem, no one to encourage me in school, and having a baby young made me desperate. My main goal in life was to land a baller. And I did just that. But it came at a great cost.

Now, I was stuck in a cell. Stuck in a position that I could've avoided. If only I had left Greer years ago, I wouldn't be in this predicament. I could've taken all the gifts he'd given me over the last few years and started a new life. A simpler life.

I shut my eyes tight, hoping that I would fall asleep. But sleep never came.

CHAPTER 15

Katya

Slowly, I walked out of the court room toward Markisa's car. My body was weary and tired from the last couple of nights. I hadn't gotten a wink of sleep while I was in jail. I hadn't had a bite to either. My despair was too great to even think of taking care of myself.

Greer had put me through the ultimate humiliation and I wasn't sure how I was going to come back from it. There was no way I could stay married to him. I had a little money saved but not enough to divorce him. Then that damn prenup would be hard to get around. I'd essentially be starting over at 35 years old. No skills. No degree. No money. Just years of being the dumb wife of a retired athlete.

I dragged my worn body to the parking lot. Markisa had bought me some make-up and a skirt suit for my preliminary hearing. Therefore I didn't look nearly as bad as I felt. The sun blazed down on my head, seemingly making a mockery out of my experience. The day was beautiful but my circumstance was hideous. I wished it was raining to match my feeling.

Markisa and her "experience" were waiting for me outside the courthouse. She was facing forward while texting on her phone. There was no doubt in mind that she was gossiping to the other wives about me. I could see her now texting, *"yeah I'm picking her pathetic ass up from jail right now."*

Exhausted, I made my way to her car and sank inside. It was the first moment I'd felt somewhat relaxed in days. That car truly was an experience. My body merged with the buttery leather seats while cool air blew from the vent.

"I go back for sentencing in a few weeks," I announced as I pulled the seatbelt across my body.

"What kind of time are you looking at?"

"None since I accepted the plea deal. Just anger management, therapy and rehab. Since I was under the influence when I attacked that raggedy bitch, my lawyer was able to get me a good deal. I'm just waiting for everything to be put into writing," I replied.

"That's good. You look like shit honey. Do you wanna go to my house to take a shower?" she asked me.

Being her decadent mansion was the last place I wanted to be.

"Nope. I just wanna go home."

"What if he's there."

"So. That's where all my shit is. I live there," I responded annoyed any her statement." He was the one that cheated. Why should I have to avoid going to my home.

"Girl..."

"Please, just take me home Markisa. I'm not in the mood for one of your lectures."

"Suit yourself. Oh I meant to tell you this. You, Jordyn and I were invited to be on Black Mecca Wives. And now that you got all this drama going on, they'll probably give you a lot of money to get on the show. This could be a new start for you. So many opportunities could arise from that. Jordyn and I definitely are going to do it. What do you think?" she asked as she drove toward my house.

"I'm not really feeling exploiting myself. Give me some time to think it over."

"Sheila, the producer, will be calling you about it in a few days."

"That'll give me time to mull it over. Thanks for letting me know." I gave Markisa a smile.

As the wheels rolled against the concrete, I fished my phone out of the plastic bag they kept my belongings in. After not being able to use it for two days, I begrudgingly hit the on button. Predictably my voicemail box was full. I had damn near 100 text messages. But the only person I wanted to speak to was my daughter. Quickly I called her to check in.

"Mom?" she answered the phone as if she were out of breath.

"Hey. I was just checking in to let you know I'm okay and on my way home. What are you up to?" I asked.

"I'm in Miami with some friends right now. We're just now leaving the beach."

"How'd you get there? Did Greer pay?" I asked, curious to know if Greer had begun cutting her off.

"No. A friend of mine paid. But you really fucked things up with Greer. He said he would agree to still pay for my tuition and rent until I graduated. He apologized to me."

"He apologized to you?!" I asked.

"Yeah. He called me that night you attacked Ashantay to explain. Look Mom, I know y'all don't get along like that. And it's low-key your fault. Your drinking has been getting worse over the last few months."

"What?" I couldn't believe what I was hearing. How could she blame me? Greer was the one in the wrong.

"Look Mom, I'm glad you're okay but I gotta go. I'll call you when I get back home," she said before hanging up.

My own daughter was blaming my husband's infidelities on me. My drinking was bad because of him. He was driving me to drink. Just like he drove me to do coke years ago. My daughter never let me live down my stint in rehab. It was only 6 weeks that I was away when she was about 15 but she brought it up often. Tears escaped down my cheek as I thought about all I had been through. I couldn't help but think of what could've been avoided had I just left Greer's trifling ass.

"Are you okay?" Markisa asked.

"No," I replied.

For the remainder of the ride, I closed my eyes and thought about everything that had just happened. I still wanted my husband dead but after threatening him in front of a crowd of people, I knew it wouldn't be the best move.

People would think that I was guilty automatically. I had to let that plan die. What was I going to do next? What were my options? My head spun in circles as we neared the house.

When I got there, the G Wagon was parked in the circle directly in front of the house. I hesitated getting out of the car, because I wasn't sure what I would be walking into.

"I know that your prenup is ironclad but I know a good lawyer that may be able to work around that. His name is John Winbush. You should give him a call," Markisa said to me as I stared out the window.

"Oh yeah?" I asked barely listening to her

"Yeah. Remember Luquoia Smith?"

"Yeah," I replied turning toward her.

"Well, she signed a prenup. She was only married for 2 years but still got to walk away with a nice settlement of $1,000,000. I know it ain't much but it's a nice nest egg to start with," Markisa encouraged.

"Text me his info."

"Okay," she replied as I hopped out of the car.

When I made my way to the door, I took a deep breath before sliding my key into the lock. I knew that I was going back into the belly of the beast. However, my key didn't fit.

"What the fuck?" I grunted.

I know this nigga did not change the locks on me.

"You okay?" Markisa yelled from the window.

I ignored her and banged the door like a mad woman. This nigga had lost his ever loving mind. He kept doing things to further drive me crazy. How could someone be so cruel, especially to their wife. When he didn't come to door after a minute of me knocking I decided I was getting in one way or another.

Pissed, I picked up one of the large pots that sat outside of the front door. The pot had an aloe vera plant inside that was about to be all over the ground. Bending my knees, I squatted really low to get a good grip on the pot. And with all of my might, I hurled it through a side window.

"KATYA!" Markisa screamed. I could hear her getting out of the car behind me. But I didn't wait for her to catch up. Instead, I jumped through the window, scratching my hand on the way in.

"Katya are you out of your mind?" I heard Greer say when he came running down the hall.

"No you are! You locked me out of my house!? What is wrong with you?!" I asked.

"I'm going to have to ask you to leave. I'm filing for a restraining order tomorrow. You are violent and erratic. Get the fuck out right now Katya!"

"Hell no! I live here!"

"Look, I'm making it easier for you. You keep both of your cars. I packed them up with as much of your shit as possible. You can come back and get the rest of your things later. I'm even giving you $100,000. It's already been deposited into your bank account. And don't worry about Zania. She'll be taken care of."

"You're really doing this to me right now? You're putting me out? As if giving me Chlamydia wasn't enough. Having two babies on me wasn't enough!"

"I'm trying to make this as amicable as possible."

"You think $100k is amicable?" I questioned, shaking my head.

"Just get out before I call the cops on you for breaking my window."

"I'm out bitch," I replied before walking out of the front door.

"Are you okay?" Markisa asked me.

"Of course not."

"Do you wanna come to my house?"

"No. I'm going to a hotel. I'll talk to you later," I replied before hopping in the G Wagon and making my way to a Kimpton hotel. I had no clue what was packed in that car but it didn't matter. It wasn't like that evil ass negro even gave me a chance pack anything.

Tears raced down my face as I drove to the hotel. The pain just wouldn't let up. It seemed as if everything was getting worse. They say when it rains it pours, but this felt like my 40 days and 40 nights of torment. But I had no ark to give me shelter to weather the storm. Instead, I was homeless. Greer is truly a piece of shit.

Eventually, I dragged my suitcase and my sad body into the hotel room. When I opened it, I noticed that Greer threw my shit in there haphazardly. This man didn't give a fuck about me on any level. There were underwear, casual clothes, a formal dress, sneakers and some stilettos I hadn't worn in years. He'd also packed some of my expensive jewelry. How generous of him.

How could you be married to someone for so long and treat them like this? It made no sense to me. I could never be this cruel to someone I once loved.

As I sat on the bed, I received a call. When I looked over at my phone, I was slightly shocked to see that it was Camden. He'd become a distant thought since all of this shit went down between me and his father. But at that moment, I was happy to hear from him. Thoughts of our tryst entered my mind, giving me some slither of joy.

"Hello?" I answered.

"Yo Kat! Are you okay? I heard about everything and I've been trying to call you. Your mailbox was full and..."

"Your father kicked me out of his house."

"Are you fuckin' kidding me?"

"No."

"Where are you now?"

"I'm at the Hotel Indigo in Downtown Atlanta. I just got here."

"Okay, I'm gonna slide through tonight. Aight? I'll bring you something to take the edge off."

"I'll see you then," I replied before hanging up.

When I got off of the phone with Camden, I decided to take a long hot shower. I wished I was still at home so that I could take a hot bath. Because there was no way I was sitting my ass in the hotel's tub.

Steam fogged the mirrors, opening my pores, giving me the detox that I needed. I watched as my grief and strife washed down the drain. I felt one hundred pounds lighter by the time I stepped out of the shower.

Quickly, I toweled off and slipped into a negligée that my husband was so kind to pack. While I waited for Camden, I ordered a burger, fries, a bottle of champagne and two bottles of wine. I was in desperate need to take the edge.

Nothing would make me happier than drowning my blues in the bottom of a bottle. But I definitely needed something to soak the alcohol up. I hadn't had a proper meal in days. And for the drinking that I planned to do, I needed something with extra carbs and fat to soak it all up.

Without having to wait that long, room service delivered my goodies. It seemed as if I took two bites of that burger before it disappeared. The fries stood no chance of being savored. And I washed it down with a bottle of Merlot.

Like a savage, I drank from the bottle because I didn't want to waste any time sipping from a glass.

Relaxation melted my cells as the wine worked its way through my body. At that moment, I gave zero fucks about Greer, Zania, Ashantay, nor her tiny bastards. I was finally carefree and relaxed.

I just wanted Camden to come through and fuck me hard so that I could further forget about my worries.

Finally he arrived. And thankfully my food had fully digested. When I opened the hotel door, my heart melted at the sight of him. His warm brown skin glowed underneath the dimly lit hall lights. He wore a crisp white t-shirt, one respectable gold chain and a pair of dark jeans.

"Come here," he said to me, opening his arms and pulling me in tightly.

He closed the door behind me and wasted no time before kissing me. "I'm sorry you had to go through that," he said as his lips pushed into mine. He didn't even give me a chance to say a word.

That was fine with me. My pussy was talking. In fact she was screaming to be filled by him. His Tom Ford cologne swallowed me whole. Against his skin it smelled like heaven.

It's funny, his father wears the same cologne. On Greer, it burns my damn nose. But on Camden it made my heartbeat.

"I been wanting to kiss you since the last time," his deep voice boomed in my ear as he slid the negligée off of my body. His lips worked on every inch of my skin available.

Everywhere they touched, tension was released. His tongue and lips glided down my neck. Sensually he nibbled and walked me back to the bed.

No words needed to be said as he spread my legs. I watched his eyes glimmer in delight of the sight of my moist cave.

"Yeah, open that pussy for me," he commanded.

I gently pulled my lips open so that he could get a glance at my pink cave. I wanted him to see how much she missed him. How much she wanted to be fucked by him.

He began to suckle my clit and I lost control. I had to take deep breaths because I felt as if I were going to prematurely come. That's how much he excited me. I was already on the brink of orgasm.

"Hmmmm." he hummed as he tasted me. The vibrations added to the sensations. And within three minutes of him suckling on my rose, I came. There was no way I could hold back. I needed that orgasm.

He ate me out until I came two more times. By the time he came up for air his beard was glistening as if he dipped it in doughnut frosting.

"Damn you wet as fuck tonight," Camden exclaimed.

"So fuck me," I said.

"I will but I'm tryna go all night again. You want some blow?" he offcrcd.

I knew it was wrong for me to take the percs the last time we were together but coke was even worse. It was my vice.

"I can't," I replied.

"Come on babe. You had a stressful week. Take the edge off with me," he pushed. The temptation was too great. And I remember how good sex used to feel when I was on coke. One little hit wasn't going to hurt nothing.

"Just a bump."

That one bump turned into two more. And before I knew it I was in the greatest ecstasy of my life.

"Ahhhh!" I cried out as Camden fucked my soul. My pussy willingly surrendered to his girth as he swam in and out of me.

I swear that boy twisted me in positions that weren't even in the Kama Sutra. The mattress had become a burst waterbed. I was so juicy that the sheets were saturated.

Trembling in ecstasy, I laid next to Camden as he puffed on a vape pen.

"Let me see that," I asked, reaching for it. I needed something to calm my heart rate down. The coke still had me energetic. It was 3am and we'd been fucking for hours.

"Here you go," he replied.

Eventually I fell asleep on top of a towel. I felt no guilt about fucking Greer's son. I just wished there was a way he could know without it coming to bite me in the ass.

CHAPTER 16

Katya

I was summoned out of my sleep by the sound of Camden's phone going off. He was already awake, sitting in the chair across from the bed. He wasn't wearing a shirt to my delight. I got to ogle his beautifully chiseled body. He did have a pair of boxers on.

"Morning," he greeted me as he reached for his phone to see who was calling.

"Morn." I smiled while reaching down to check my phone.

"Aye wsup... Yeah I got you. I'll be there a little later," he said while hanging up.

"You're about to leave me?" I asked.

"I got moves to make but I can come back later. We still have a lot to talk about," he said while standing up.

I watched as his muscular frame slipped into a pair of jeans and his t-shirt. He moved as if he were floating on air. Every time I saw his muscles or his jaw flex, I was reminded of the unsurmountable pleasure he brought me last night. I was still tingling from head to toe. But I was severely dehydrated from the coke and the liquor.

"What did you want to talk about?" I asked. I sat up from the bed with sheet draping over my titties.

"My father. I know you want him gone now more than ever. I mean sure, we're gonna have to give some money to his baby moms once he's dead but we'll still get a lot."

"Fuck. Oh shit…" I turned my head to the side. I wanted to back out of the deal we made. After my assault charge there was no way I was going help kill Greer. They would certainly investigate my ass first. And after those two nights in jail, I knew I wasn't cut out for a lifelong prison sentence.

Besides, if the Black Mecca Wivesshow, becomes real for me, then I wouldn't need Greer's money anyway. I also wanted to talk to that lawyer about the divorce. Even though I wanted Greer to pay for what he put me through. Killing him wasn't the way to go through with it.

"What is it?" Camden asked.

"We can't kill Greer," I conceded.

"Why not? You got cold feet?"

"Camden, I know that your father is a rat bastard. And I wish to God that a lightning bolt would strike down from heaven into his chest but we can't kill him. I don't want to go to prison and I'm hot right now. I got this assault charge. People heard me threaten him in the hospital. It just doesn't seem like a wise move."

"Are you kidding me right now?" he asked. I could see the malice brewing behind his eyes. He looked as if I were denying him entry into heaven. As if I had stolen something dire to his survival. Perhaps I had.

"No. Listen, you're smart. And young. Just build a relationship with him and he'll eventually come around and help you with your business."

"No the fuck he won't Katya. This the same nigga that had twins on you! Same nigga that threw you out on your ass. You his wife. He ain't gon' do shit for me. Yo his insurance money is the only way for me to get out of my rut. Aight? I ain't got no other options."

"I'm sorry Camden. I just can't help you. But believe me, if he died, I would split the money with you in a heartbeat. You deserve it more than anyone," I tried to reason with him. But judging my by the dead look behind his eyes, I knew it wasn't working.

"Whatever. I got shit to do today. I see why he fucked you over. Because he knew you ain't got no backbone. I'm out. And you can have the rest of this," he said while tossing the baggie of coke onto the bed.

"Camden don't be like that," I called out to him but he waved me off and slammed the door behind him.

He would be okay though. We all would. Moments after he left, I took another hot shower and ordered breakfast as well as a carafe of mimosa. I knew that it was reckless to drink that much by myself in the morning but I deserved it. I'd been through so much.

By the time I'd finished breakfast and half of the carafe, I decided to email the divorce lawyer that Markisa recommended. Within a flash, he responded asking me if I could come in for a 15 minute consultation later that day. I had nothing better to do.

Within two hours, I was dressed and ready to meet the lawyer. When I spoke to John Winbush on the phone he asked me to bring a copy of my prenup. Fortunately, I had a copy saved in my email. But at some point I needed to get back in the house to get my laptop since it had a lot of my other important files.

Winbush, Cramer, and Associates was located downtown where there was absolutely no parking nor valet. I was annoyed that I had to park in a garage, especially since the only decent shoes to go with my outfit were a pair of thigh high boots with a 6 inch heel.

Slowly, I walked toward his office building so that I could see if I had a real case. On the way there I prayed that there was a loophole. I was so stupid to sign that damn thing. I remember doing it out of desperation. I wanted to prove to him that I wasn't marrying him for his money.

"Katya?" I heard a voice call my name as I neared the law office.

When I turned to see who was calling me, I noticed it was Davis. Greer's concierge doctor.

"Hey Davis," I greeted him with opening my arms for a hug.

"Wow, in spite of everything you still look stunning. How're you holding up baby girl?" he sweetly asked me as we stepped to the side to let pedestrians walk by.

"I'm hanging on by a thread. But I'm on my way to see a divorce attorney," I nervously laughed.

"I hope you drain that nigga. He's a piece of shit for what he put you through. If I had a woman like you…" he shook his head while sexily grinning at me.

I grew nervous under his stare. His words were flattering because I believed him. Davis had been low-key flirting with me for years but I was always faithful to my bitch-ass husband. I'd always been attracted to Davis but was stern about not acting on it.

"Davis you always saying some sweet shit."

"I mean it. Let me take you out."

"What about that chick from the party?" I asked him.

"Who? Kelly? That wasn't serious. We're not even seeing each other anymore. I put that on my mama's grave," he said while holding up his hand.

"I don't know. I'm dealing with a lot right now."

"It's just dinner. I just wanna show you a good night out. No pressure. Just you and me looking over the water while sharing some lobster."

"I'll think about it."

"Take your time. I'll be waiting on your call. Good luck at your meeting," he said before giving me another hug and kiss on the cheek.

A warm and fuzzy feeling spread throughout my body as I continued over to the office building. Davis was fine and always nice to me. I wished I had met someone like him back in my early 20s. I should've been in college meeting men like him. Instead, I was broken, damaged and in survival mode trying to pull a baller.

I shook my head as I thought of my past transgressions. Moments later I was sitting across from John Winbush, esquire talking about my potential divorce case.

"And you were in rehab when?" he asked as he looked over my prenup.

"Four years ago."

"How long would you say you were suffering from substance abuse? 16 years?" he asked.

"No, I wouldn't say that long..."

"No it was 16 years," he reiterated while staring at me with intensity. John was an older man who looked as if he might be mixed. If it weren't for the loose curls atop his head, he could pass for white. His green eyes burrowed into my soul as he waited for me to respond.

Then it clicked. I knew exactly what he was getting it.,

"Let's say 16 years."

"Can other people attest for your drug use and alcohol abuse back then?"

"Yeah."

"So you were intoxicated when you signed this. You have a history of drug and substance abuse. You've gotten help for it once. You've just been remanded by the court to get help from it again. It's been an ongoing problem with you. And when you signed this, you were under the influence. Thus it's null and void," he said while leaning back in his leather chair in satisfaction.

"Just like that?" I cocked my head to the side.

"Oh we'll have to go to trial. I'll need evidence that you were using back then. But that's easy. I can get this ripped up. You'd have access to half of his wealth. And to be honest, you had to be high when you signed this," he shook his head.

"I know." I was ashamed. Back when we got married, everyone was telling me how dumb I was for signing it but I was desperate. Without much to my name, I didn't feel like I had any choices.

"I would never let my daughter sign something like this. But don't worry, you're going to be taken care of when I'm through with him."

"How much do I have to pay you for retainer?"

"$15k. But don't worry, we'll sue him for your lawyer fees and court costs," he smiled at me.

I let out a breath of relief as I extended my hand to thank him.

"I'll get everything filed within a week. You're well on your way to being a free woman."

"That's the best news I've gotten in a long time."

"I'm happy to help you out. We're gonna hit that cheating bastard right where it hurts. I'll be in touch."

Joy flooded my entire spirt as I damn near skipped out of that law office. While I felt bad about Camden. I was so happy that I would finally get my happily ever after. Who knew there would be a benefit to doing drugs and drinking.

I decided that once the settlement was complete, I would give Camden a million dollars. That's what he originally wanted. I'd feel bad if I came out of this with $50 million, plus half of Greer's property and Camden was left with nothing.

As I marched back to my car, I received a call.

"Hello?"

"Is this Katya Song?"

"This is she."

"Hey Katya. This is Sheila Jessup. I'm the producer for Black Mecca Wives. Listen, I'm sorry about what you're going through but it was brought to my attention. I think you'd be a great fit into the show. I know that you're friends with Jordyn Johns and Markisa Randolph. They've already agreed to do the show. We're currently scouting other wives but I'd like to center the first season around you and your husband's drama."

"You know before when Markisa mentioned I was like no. I don't want to exploit my hardships. But I want the world to know how trifling my husband is. I want them to know my struggles as a single mother and why I chose him. I had a rough life. I have a story to tell," I stated firmly.

"Yes you do. And that story can make you a lot of money. So let's meet for a test shoot in a couple of days. I'm in town for a week before I have to head back to LA. I'm sure the test shoot will go well because you are gorgeous."

"Sounds good to me. You can send me the details..." I said to her before giving her my email address.

When we got off the phone, I felt like a weight had been lifted off of my chest. I was the victor in the end.

CHAPTER 17

Camden

Just when I thought that I had a clear path to an abundance of money, I came to a dead end. I felt as if I had come down from a glorious high and crashed into a dark hole. Fucking Katya left me intoxicated, but her telling me she didn't want to kill my pops left me numb.

I clenched my jaw as I rode in the back of my Uber, pissed that she was reneging on our plan. She had no clue that I was running around without a car, with a baby on the way, and a slew of debts. Not to mention I had to fight an assault charge because of my dumbass baby mother, Naija. The stress kept piling on top of me and I felt like I was gonna snap if I didn't get a grip.

Katya probably hadn't heard about me getting arrested since she'd been involved in a criminal charge herself. I couldn't lie, when I heard about her fucking up my pops' side bitch, I laughed. Too bad she ain't fuck him up instead. But I knew that it wasn't a smart move. She was right about it making her look hot. If my pops were to die right now, they would blame her. And that could work in my favor. They wouldn't suspect me at all. To the public eye, my pops and I had a low-key relationship. I never blasted him for cutting me off.

I remained private about our relationship issues because I knew that if I went live, he would cut off communication. I thought that if I could at least remain in his ear there was a chance that he would help me out again. But he'd proven yet again that he didn't give a fuck about me.

Annoyed, I stared out of the window while plotting my next moves. Tonight Marco and I were going to finally be enacting our plan to rob Cray's mother's house. The cash from that robbery would hold me down for a little while but ultimately I needed a real large lump sum. I needed at least $1 million to make some serious moves.

Moments later, I was dropped off at my condo. Frustrated, I made my way into my spot. I was pissed at Katya, but thoughts of fucking her kept coming back to mind. She was the best I'd ever had but I couldn't let that cloud my judgement. I had to find a way to convince her to help me take out my pops. And if she wouldn't get on board I'd get at him myself.

After I settled at my spot, I rolled a joint, ordered some food and decompressed until it was time to meet Marco. Marco and I had been planning this robbery over the last few days. I knew all about Cray's mother's security system. I knew that she didn't turn on the alarm until she was about to go to bed which was around midnight. We decided to cut the alarm phone lines, right after midnight. The jewelry that Cray bought her was kept in a bedroom that was converted into a walk in closet. We'd be in and out in 5 minutes tops.

We planned on bringing guns to intimidate her but we knew we wouldn't have to use them. This was a small price that Cray would have to pay for being famous and fucking over his best friend.

If you would've told me years ago that I would've been willing to rob my best friend's mother, I would've slapped you for the insinuation. Ms. Vanessa had been a second mother to me. She and my mother were like sisters. I'd kill a nigga for robbin' my mother.

But a nigga was getting desperate. And since he cut me off, it was hard to give a fuck about his needs and desires. After all we had been through he was supposed to hold me down. Since he's decided to become an enemy, I was going to treat him like one.

Day faded into night as I began anticipate pulling off this heist. My nerves began to tangle because I knew that it was wrong. There was a part of me that wanted to call it off. Cray ain't deserve that shit. Ms. Vanessa ain't never did nothing to me but show me love.

At 10:00pm, Marco showed up. Feeling confused and regretful, I went to open the door for him. He was dressed in all black with a ski mask gripped in his hand. I could tell he was ready to go to work but I was having doubts.

"Why you not dressed?" he asked when he saw me in my white tee and grey sweats.

"I was just thinkin'..."

"You tryna' back out of it?" he asked, with frustration written on his face.

"Ms. Vanessa is family. I can't do that to her. Let's just call it off," I replied.

As soon as the words left my mouth, Rayvon called me.

"Fuck..." I grunted before answering the phone. "Wsup?"

"Yo baby boy, you forget about me?" he asked. I cringed at him calling me baby boy, especially since I knew what he does on his free time.

"Nah. I'm working on it."

"I'ma need a payment tonight. You feel me? I been letting you slide but I need something a.s.a.p. before I go visit Naija." There was a small part of me that wanted to tell him to go ahead and visit that bitch. But she was still carrying my seed. As angry as I was at her, I didn't want anything to happen to my baby.

"Aight. I'll meet you around 2:00am," I said before hanging up.

"So what's it going to be?" Marco asked me.

"I ain't got no choice."

Rayvon was the reminder that I needed. That nigga put the fire back under me to go through with my heinous plan. Ms. Vanessa was gonna be alright though. She had insurance. I know that I would always feel guilty about what I did to her, but desperate times call for desperate measures.

"You had me worried there for a second," Marco laughed as he pulled out a pistol. He handed it to me. Shaking my head, I looked down at it. *It's just to intimidate her, nothing more.* I thought to myself.

On the drive to Vanessa's place, my stomach churned making me feel nauseous. I just knew that at any moment I was going to throw up all over Marco's whip. He let the windows down but that didn't help cool me off. Sweat poured from me as he sped down the road. Finally we arrived in her neighborhood.

Right after midnight Marco and I were outside of Ms. Vanessa's house. The street was bare of any cars or pedestrians. There were no cars in her driveway. I assumed they were in the garage. I secretly prayed no one was in the house. That would be even better. It was a Saturday night, she could be out.

"Shine your phone light over here," Marco requested so that he could cut the chords.

Once we were done making sure the alarms wouldn't go off, we made our way through the back of the house. My heart pounded in my chest as I kicked in the glass door. A voice deep inside kept yelling at me to turn around and go home but I couldn't stop. I needed this money badly.

Together Marco and I made our way through the house. The lights were all off and Vanessa wasn't anywhere on the first floor. There was some relief when I realized she might not be home.

Because of my nerves my throat was dry and scratchy. I felt the urge to cough but held it back so that I wouldn't make any noise. I took deep breaths as we moved through the house, making our way to the stairs.

"I'm about to get some water," I heard Vanessa say but I didn't hear anyone respond. I assumed she was on the phone.

"Fuck!" I whispered.

"Shhhh!" Marco turned around and placed his finger over his mouth.

We knew that if she walked up on us, that one of us would subdue her and go get the jewels. As soon as she made her way off of the stairs, she jumped when she saw us.

"AHHHH!" she screamed.

"Shut the fuck up!" Marco yelled while aiming the gun at her head.

"Please don't hurt me," she whimpered.

I immediately felt horrible. This was a woman who has cooked for me. She's picked me up from school. Allowed me to sleep in her home. I felt terrible that we were doing this to her.

"Bitch we don't wanna hurt you! Take us to the jewelry!" he demanded as he walked her toward the stairs. Aggressively he pushed while aiming the gun at her head. I followed behind them as we made our way to our closet.

"Oh my God! " Vanessa yelled as we made our way up the stairs. When we got on the floor, someone else was standing at the end of the hallway. It was another woman. She fired a shot toward us and the bullet landed into Marco's leg.

"Fuck! Bitch!" Marco screamed while grabbing his leg with one hand and shooting toward the figure in the hall. The person fell back on the ground instantly. It was wild how both Marco and the other person could see enough to get a shot.

But I was disoriented. I'd completely underestimated that someone else would be in the house and that there would be a gun involved.

"CARINA, NO!" Vanessa screamed.

"Mama?" I stupidly asked. I was stunned that my mother was there this late. And she was the one with the gun.

Outraged, I raced toward her and fell to knees. "Mama!" I cried out.

"Camden?" Vanessa asked.

POP POP

Marco fired two shots in Vanessa before he turned on the lights. Vanessa laid on the ground with two wounds to the head while my mother was on the floor with a wound to the chest. Neither of them were moving or breathing.

"WHAT THEF FUCK!?!?! You killed my mother! Mama!!!" I hollered while holding her close. Tears immediately purged from my eyes as I watched her bleed out.

"Nigga she shot me first. And then this one... she knew who you were. I ain't goin' to prison over this shit. Where's the jewelry?" Marco callously asked but I was too shocked to think.

He eventually walked away and barged into the rooms until he found the one he was looking for. I sat on the floor holding my mother closely. Both of the women were dressed in robes which I found odd. I knew they were close but I never thought their relationship was more than a friendship. There was a part of me that wanted to pick that gun up and turn it on to myself.

"Come on I got everything. We gotta get out of here!" he Marco said while pulling me up from my mother.

Tears raced down my face through the mask as he pulled me out of the house. Everything after that moment was a blur. I'm not even sure how I made it home. But I wished that Marco had shot me instead.

CHAPTER 18

Katya

For the first time in a long while, I slept like a baby last night. A bottle of wine, knocked me out for at least 12 hours and it was glorious. Yesterday was the best day that I'd had in a long time. Finding out that I could challenge the prenup and possibly win, gave me so much hope. And knowing that I would be on the reality show was the cherry on top.

Sunlight pierced through the slit in between the heavy shades on the hotel room. Just that little line of light beaming on my face, was enough to tug my eyelids open. Grateful that I had the entire bed to myself, I stretched like a starfish and smiled.

It was my first genuine smile in almost two months. Ever since Greer had given me a STD, I'd been feeling low and depressed. But knowing that I was going to be fine without him brought me immense joy.

As soon as I got out of bed, I took a shower and then ordered breakfast. While I waited on my breakfast, I decided to call Tyshawn to see if he had time to do my make-up on short notice. Tonight I was doing a test shoot with Jordyn, Markisa and few other women. Ty was the only person I trusted to hook my face up to perfection.

"Of course I can do your beat. Send me the address!"

"Okay!" I said before hanging up. I then called Latonia to make sure she was available to hook up my hair.

Once all of that was done, I ate my breakfast and enjoyed being alone in my hotel room. I felt awful about reneging on the agreement I made with Camden but I vowed to myself to give him some money once I receive a settlement. Greer was a piece of shit and I wanted him to pay for how he treated me and his son.

While I lounged and had breakfast in bed, I received a call from Davis. I perked up and answered his call.

"Hey you," I warmly greeted.

"Hey beautiful. You sound cheerful. What's going on?"

"Well, my meeting with the lawyer went well. And I'll be doing a test shoot for Black Mecca Wives. So, I'm on cloud nine right now."

"That's awesome. I'm happy for you! Damn make sure you save time for dinner with me."

"I'm free tomorrow but we gotta be low key. I don't want this getting back to Greer. He cannot win in this divorce," I replied.

"Oh that's fine. I can hire a private chef and we can eat here. Or I can whisk you away. Take you out a private beach. How's that sound?"

"That's sounds good. Davis, you've always been so kind to me…"

"I don't know if you know this but you were really there for me when my wife died. I remember you sending over cooked meals and calling to check on me. I know you did it out of the kindness of your heart but it really touched me and my Michelle," he said referring to his daughter.

"You're welcome. I just felt so bad for you two, especially Michelle. A teenage girl losing her mother is awful. I lost mine when I was 17. We didn't have a good relationship though. But it still hurt."

"How'd she die if you don't mind me asking?"

"Car accident. She was drunk and driving. Zania was almost 2 at the time. I was left on my own to figure out everything," I replied.

My mother wasn't a big help with Zania though. The most she did was allow us to still live with her. Her death was actually a blessing because of the insurance money.

"Wow, I'm sorry to hear that. There's a lot I don't know about you Kat, but I really want to learn."

"We can take our time and get to know each other. But I have to go. My make-up artist and hairstylist will be here at any second."

"Okay, I'll start planning for our little getaway. Have fun and uh, break a leg? Would you say that for a reality show?"

"Probably not since bitches are known to fight. I don't want anyone breaking my leg," I laughed.

"Me either. I'll talk to you later," he laughed before hanging up.

An hour later, my stylists were in my hotel, beautifying me. As Tyshawn beat my face, Latonia made sure my coif was laid. It felt good to be pampered with a purpose. I was determined to go far with this reality show.

I decided I was going to write a book about my experiences, start a boutique, get into real estate and investments. I was coming out of this divorce a boss. My husband could no longer hold me down.

"You look amazing!" Latonia complimented.

"Mmmmhmmm," Tyshawn echoed.

His attitude had been off the entire time he was doing my make-up but I didn't think much of it. In fact, I didn't care. I was in a blissful mood now that everything was turning around for me.

"Are you okay?" Latonia asked.

"Man problems..." he said while shaking my head.

"She knows that all too well," Latonia joked in my direction.

"I don't even want to think about it. Just know that you're young and free. You don't have to accept less than what you deserve," I said to him before standing up to check myself out in the mirror.

"I know. I'ma be okay," he smiled while packing up his kit.

After I paid them, they headed out and I got dressed. I slipped into a black jumpsuit that hugged my curves, a pair of Fendi ankle boots and with a matching purse. My blonde bob was laid and feathered to perfection. My make-up was HD camera ready. And my confidence was finally on 100.

I drove my car to the lounge where we were all supposed to meet. And when I walked in, Markisa was the first person I saw. She looked beautiful, dressed in a zebra print dress with a pair of yellow Louboutin's and a bright red lip.

"Hey girl! You look well rested!" Markisa commented when she saw me.

The last time we were together, I was throwing a vase through a window. She'd just rescued me from jail. I probably looked like a cat that I got stuck in a dryer when she came to get me. I avoided mirrors because I knew that I looked rough. I didn't want to add to my despair by seeing how ugly was. But now I looked and felt good.

"Yes! I feel much better."

"You talked to John?" she asked while nudging me playfully.

"Yep!"

"Told you that nigga could hook you up. I just need two more years in my raggedy ass marriage before I hire him," she laughed.

"What?" I knew that he cheated but I didn't know she was thinking about leaving him.

"Yeah. 10 years of marriage voids our prenup. And John can help me get whatever I desire," she laughed.

"I ain't mad at ya."

Moments later, we were all sitting around the dinner table for our test shoot. Sheila stood in the back with the directors and camera crews while we all talked and drank.

"So does everyone know each other?" Markisa asked.

I only knew her and Jordyn. There were other women I was familiar with but I didn't know them personally.

"No, let's introduce ourselves," I announced. "I'm Katya Song, soon to be ex-wife of former pro-footballer Greer Song."

Eventually all of them women introduced themselves. The last woman was someone I'd seen around but hadn't ever spoken too.

"I'm Jessica Trudeau. I'm the ex-girlfriend Charles McGants, Ricky Mariano and Greer Song."

Record scratch. This is the drama that the show wanted out of us. Who was this bitch that dated Greet.

"When did you date Greer?" Jordyn pried. I could tell she was instigating. It was as if she was getting wet from the impending drama.

"We had a 6 month fling about five years ago. He bought me a ring and told me he was leaving his wife but that never happened. I recognize how I wrong I was and I'm sorry Katya," she said while looking over at me.

All eyes were on me. I could feel my chest tightening as their orbs zeroed in on my face. Heat flushed my entire body and I had half the mind to lift this table up and flip it over. I was already a bottle of wine in and I wasn't in the mood for any bullshit.

"You fucked with him, knowing he was married?" I asked, looking at her intently.

"Listen girl, Greer is for everybody. That nigga is a certified hoe. A generous hoe. But a hoe, nonetheless. He belongs to the streets. I don't know why you tried to turn him into a husband. But I guess, hoes of a feather..." before she could even finish her statement I hurled my glass toward her.

Luckily for her the bitch had quick reflexes and she ducked.

"Oooh this is good. Are you getting this?" I heard Sheila ask in the background.

Quickly, I jumped up and charged toward Jessica ready to rip her tacky ass wig off her head. The shit was sitting on her head like a helmet. I hated when bitches didn't blend the lace in.

Before I could land more than one hit, the bodyguards had pulled me off of her.

"Go cool off, Kat," Sheila said to me.

"This is why you brought me here? So that I could fight?" I asked.

"Look, we brought you here, because we knew you had some drama. It's okay. You're going to make money off it. This is just the test shoot it won't always be like this."

"Fuck this. I'm out," I announced as I turned and walked away.

"Get her walking out!" Sheila yelled at the cameraman.

"Katya!" Markisa called after me.

I ignored her and kept stomping away until I made it back to my car. Hot tears flooded my face as I thought about the constant humiliation. Everywhere I turned there was another bitch that my husband had fucked while he was still married to me.

My life was a joke. I would never be anything more than the dumb bitch that stayed married to a male whore. As the tears soaked my face, I drove to another bar several blocks away.

Once I was there, I parked my ass at the bar and asked for gin. I was good on wine for the night. I needed the strong shit. I needed to forget about my problems for a little bit.

Alcohol had become my only real friend. Markisa wasn't a friend. My humiliation was her entertainment. But alcohol wasn't entertained by my pain. It just listened and then soothed me. There was no judgment, just comfort and escapism.

I was in so much pain and turmoil from what my husband had put me through. An assault charge, STD, public humiliation and fights. And I degraded myself by sleeping with his son. I hated Greer for putting me through this. I hated myself for staying. I wished he were dead. I wished that could suffer like I'd been suffering.

"I think that's your last one," the bartender said to me after several drinks.

Those were the last words I remembered until I woke up the next morning in my hotel bed. My head banged as if someone was inside punching my brain. My stomach felt sour and my mouth was drier than the Sahara.

"How the fuck did I get home?" I wondered as I dragged my tired body out of the bed.

As soon as I stood to my feet, I heard a knock on the door. It sounded as if someone had set off bombs. It probably wasn't that loud because of my intense hangover, all sounds were magnified.

"Who the fuck could that be?" I asked as I looked through the peephole and saw a woman and man.

"Who is it?"

"The police," the man responded while showing his badged.

"Yes?" I asked annoyed when I opened the door.

"Katya Song?"

"Yeah, I'm Katya."

"We need to talk to you. Your husband Greer Song was found murdered early this morning."

"What?" My heart stopped in my chest. Greer was dead? It was surreal and my heart couldn't believe it. My aching head grew light and everything went black.

To be continued...

For sneak peaks, giveaways and contests, join my group! >>> http://bit.ly/NDiaRaeGroup

Would you like to be notified of part 2...

TEXT NDIA to 900900

Join my mailing list >>> http://bit.ly/5starlitmaillist

Follow me on IG

The Side N*gga Next Door

There's something about a hidden affair that makes the sex that much more exciting. Secret dick made your pussy so much more juicy than the run of the mill, day after day dick from your man. Of course when you get some new dick, you feel exhilarated but when you're keeping it from your friends, your family, your son, and your *husband,* it means that much more. The shit was hypnotizing!

"Damn Toni," her secret lover whispered while she swiveled her hips and rocked back and forth on all 10 inches of his vascular, pulsating dick.

She succulently licked her lips and tossed her head back while running her pink ombre stiletto nails through her short pixie cut. He stroked the length of her spine with one hand while the other held her wide wild hips. The lovers' eyes locked before Toni knelt down and planted a kiss on his lips.

This was her personal heaven. Having her back blown out in the late afternoon on a set of 1000 thread Egyptian cotton sheets while a ceiling fan swirled above was the pinnacle of her dry ass week. If only this feeling could last all day, every day, she wished to herself.

Her faithful doting husband, Ace, was out of town visiting his family and he wouldn't be home for a few more hours. Her son was away in California visiting his grandparents for spring break. He wasn't going to return until later that night. Therefore she and her little secret had some time to get it in.

"Choke me," she moaned between pumps.

Without hesitation he brought his hands to her neck and began squeezing firmly. Air escaped her lungs and the tightening sensation in her throat sent her flying high. Toni's heartbeat sped up as he choked her harder. He began pumping his dick in and out of her cave, thrashing at her g-spot.

"Yea take that shit," he grunted while fucking her hard.

Sweat poured from her pores and the whirling fan did nothing to keep her dry. Their damp bodies collided into one another passionately and she could feel herself about to squirt all over him.

Unable to hold her body up any longer, she toppled over on him, her 36 double ds pressing into his chiseled chest. She sank her teeth into his ripped shoulder while his hands clutched her ass. He pumped in and out, showing no mercy.

"Shit!" She moaned.

"Come for me, Toni," he spoke.

Unable to hold back any longer, she squirted like a Super Soaker, marinating the sheets. *Fuck, I'm going to have to change the sheets before Ace gets home,* she thought to herself as she laid on top of her mystery man's chest.

"Suck it for me," he commanded as she laid there lazily.

She rolled her eyes while mustering up the strength to fill her jaws with all of his girth. That orgasm had exhausted her of any dick-sucking energy but since he came through and blew her back out, she guessed she had to return the favor.

The girth of his dick stretched her pouty mouth wide. She could feel the spit spilling from the sides of her lips as she gobbled his dick like it was a hot dog at a cookout on the fourth of July. His strong ass hands gripped the back of her head and she had to push his hand away.

With how she and her husband's finances were set up, she wasn't sure when she was going to be able to get her hair redone. So, she needed that nigga to stop fuckin' her 'do up. She continued to suck him until he busted his sweet nut down her throat.

"DAMN!" He barked while punching the mattress. By the way he reacted when they fucked, Toni could tell she was the best sex that he had ever had.

She maneuvered off of him and laid down on the bed, staring up at the fan. *This man had some good dick*, she thought to herself.

"You tryna go again?" he asked her.

"No, I gotta clean up before Ace gets back here. Don't you have work to do?" she responded.

"Yea I got some shit to handle but I'd rather stay here and please you."

"As good as that sounds, you have to leave," She said as she sat up from the bed. Butt nakedly, she hopped up and put on her merlot colored satin robe. But despite making moves, this nigga laid in her bed, nestled underneath the covers as if it were his. If he thinks he's about to take a nap in her shit, he had another thing coming.

The hell does he think he doing? She thought to myself before marching over to him and snatching the duvet off of his naked body, revealing his muscular chocolate frame. His deep dark skin glistened from their after sex glow and if she weren't afraid of getting caught she would have hopped right back on his dick and rode him again.

"The fuck Toni?" He snapped before jumping up.

"I told you, you have to go." She stood with one hand on her hip as she eyed him closely.

"You're a fuckin' trip," he replied.

"Watch how you talk to me," she said.

He only shook his head and began to pull his Calvin Klein boxers up, putting away his delicious dick. Such a shame she didn't get to suck a little while longer but if her husband comes in here and witnesses this, he will have her and this nigga killed.

"When can I fuck you again?" he asked while pulling his jeans up, followed by his shirt over his head. He was putting away her favorite buffet, she thought to myself as his abs and chest were suddenly all concealed.

"I don't know but as soon as I get some time you'll be the first to know," she replied. As bad as she wanted to rip his clothes off as soon as possible, she had to remain cool. There was no way she could let this affair become her addiction.

That's where cheaters mess up, they let their affairs become priority in their lives over their marriages.

At this point she still had a level head and didn't make too many bad choices. She tried not to fuck him too often so that her husband didn't become suspicious. But since her husband wasn't in town she decided to get it in all weekend. Now that Ace was returning today in a few hours, this nigga had to go.

"Aight, well I'll be waiting for that call," her mystery man said while whispering in her ear. He pulled her in close by her hips before kissing her sensually. That kiss sent fireworks throughout her body and she had half the mind to fuck again. Instead, she kissed him back and broke away from his clutch.

She walked him down the stairs and gave him a hug goodbye before he walked out of her door. Now, she had to do the laundry and replace the covers before Ace returned.

Before going upstairs, she stopped in the living room and admired Ace's wall of accolades. She looked at how far they've fallen from glory. Viewing what once was, she shook her head in disappointment.

Her husband Ace used to be a professional boxer. Iron Ace, is what they used to call him. Back then he was swole, had swag and had money! Well, now he was thin, broke, blind and bound to a wheelchair. After a damaging blow to the head, he lost his memory for a while, his sight, and his ability to walk. The doctors said that he may be able to see and walk one day but after six years, that nigga was still like a crippled Ray Charles. But his memory did come back.

She and Ace met at a night club 15 years ago at the height of his career. He and his boys were lit as fuck in a VIP section while she and her best friend Alexia were on the dance floor looking like two bad bitches. Alexia and Toni looked so good while twerking on the floor, Ace had his bodyguard bring them to VIP. That night changed both of their lives forever.

Alexia hooked up with Ace's ex-manager and best-friend, Zeus and eventually married him. Ace and Toni dated for a few months before she got pregnant and he made her wifey. At the time she was in college studying to become a teacher and had 2 more years to graduate. Ace respected that she had something going for herself so he encouraged her to finish. And despite being a new mother she finished on time. He said she didn't have to work if she didn't want to once they were married but that having a degree was the smart thing to do.

Toni graduated right after he wifed her but she didn't work. Instead, she became the best trophy wife and stay at home mom a rich man could afford. Her 15 year old son Xavier was the light of her life and when she wasn't focused on looking good, she was focused on making sure Xavier had the best education, training for football, clothes, and other fun experiences. But now that they were struggling for money she had to cut back on what she gave to Xavier which made her resent Ace.

But back when she put in work to become a trophy wife she started with her looks. While she was already a bad bitch, she decided to get a little plastic surgery, all on Ace's dime of course.

She had c-cups but upgraded them to d's. And her ass was already thick with matching hips, but her waist wasn't as small as she'd like it to be. Therefore, she flew out to the Dominican Republic, against US doctor's orders, and got a couple of ribs removed and a tummy tuck a la Keisha Kaior. Before she knew it, she looked like Jessica Rabbit and Halley Berry had a baby. Her butterscotch skin and heart shaped face made the hearts of men melt. But she was all Ace's, until a few months ago.

Ace loved the new look but he swore he loved her no matter what. He bought her anything her heart desired. Toni's closet was filled with minks, $1000 shoes, silk, Italian leather and the best couture out of Europe. The sexy couple traveled the world to the most secluded places; Ibiza, the Maldives, the Seychelles and even Guam. Life was better than any bitch from Southeast D.C. could have hoped for. And when that all changed she was crushed!

Ace went from being one of the wealthiest athletes in the world to being damn near a joke. Unbeknownst to her he was taking care of his entire family! And not talking just his mama. No; all FIVE of his siblings, their families and several people in his entourage. On top of all of that he invested in bad business deals. So when he lost his sight and ability to walk, he lost almost everything.

Toni stayed because the doctors thought his sight would return and that he would be mobile, but now she's pissed and bitter that it hasn't. Gone are the days where they ate out almost every night, rubbed elbows with Hollywood's elite and lived in a gargantuan mansion.

Now they were confined to a modest townhouse in the suburbs of Maryland where she was his primary caregiver. They could only afford a physical therapist at the time but not health aide. The physical therapist was convinced that he would walk again but Toni had given up hope.

Most of her expensive clothes and jewels were sold. And to make matters worse , she had to take her lazy ass to work! Something she thought she would never have to do. Thank God she got her college degree. She was currently working as a high school english teacher not too far from where their home is. It was embarrassing when she had to return to being a normal basic bitch.

The whispers behind her back and in the gossip blogs became unbearable and drove her into a deep depression. It even caused her to have a miscarriage. Ace became depressed and soon after they stopped having sex. She couldn't afford to divorce him and live on her own so she stayed, miserable as fuck.

After 6 years of no real sex, she started sleeping with her secret lover only a few months ago. And honestly, it's the most exhilarated she'd felt in a long time. For now, she had no plans on leaving her husband. He still made money by doing public speaking appearances around the country. He also runs a non-profit community center for at risk youth in Southeast, D.C. That's commendable and all, but that shit don't pay the bills. He's giving his time and what little bit of money he has to those little niggas when his wife has to shop at Ross!

This is part of the reason she cheated on him. He wasn't making her a priority. It's always "Toni I need to give back to the community..." What about her?! She was his community! He couldn't even fuck her anymore and now she was fed up.

As she thought about how her life had taken a nose dive she walked past a mirror that hung on the wall in the living room. When she looked at herself, she became disappointed in what she saw. Her eyes looked tired and old and her skin was dry since she could no longer afford facials and spa days. Her once tiny waist had expanded and her Jessica Rabbit body was soon to be a Mrs. Butterworth body. However, with a pair of Spanx, she still had an hour glass shape.

She dyed her short pixie cut hair raven black because she loved the contrast between her warm skin and that dark color. Her eyes were the shade amber, which Ace said hypnotized him when he first looked into them. Now that nigga can't even see them.

At 34, she had lived to see a lot of shit. She wasn't ready to settle down and stay the lame ass wife of a blind paraplegic ass nigga. She still had some good years left in this body to be treated the way that she thought she deserved. She knew that she and her current side piece can't ever become official. But she was open to the possibility of someone else coming in and wifing her the way that she deserved.

She believed it was a man's duty to shower his lady with every thing her heart desires. And the fact that Ace couldn't do that shit for her, enraged her.

Rather than mope around the house, feeling sorry for herself, she quickly stripped the bed and begun doing the laundry. Currently, it was spring break so she decided to go ahead and began grading papers from the midterms she gave before vacation.

When she stripped the sheets from her mattress, she got a whiff of her lover's cologne and it caused a surge of sensation to shoot through her pussy. *Damn, I wish I could fuck him again, just once more before Mr. Magoo comes back home,* she thought to herself.

To read more download "The Side N*gga Next Door" Today!

5STARLIT
PRESENTS
The Side
NIGGA
Next Door
N'DIA RAE

www.ingramcontent.com/pod-product-compliance
Lightning Source LLC
Chambersburg PA
CBHW071619150726
48000CB00004B/1796